"You did love me once, Cathy."

Anthony's hand slid caressingly to her nape. "Give it a chance," he breathed with a husky longing.

"No." The cry broke from her lips, an instinctive reaction to a time of such torment. *Let the past stay in the past,* she determined with panicky resolution, thinking of Tom and all he'd done for her.

"No two people in the world have loved so totally as we did." Anthony gently pulled her into his arms, holding her with a tenderness that made her tremble. "It can be different for us now, but if it would make you happier to walk away, then do it."

He stopped dancing. His hands slid down to hers, a fingertip grasp that held her there more strongly than any embrace. The choice was hers. She could walk away—build a life with Tom. But did she want to?

EMMA DARCY nearly became an actress until her fiancé declared he preferred to attend the theater *with* her. She became a wife and mother. Later she took up oil painting—unsuccessfully, she remarks. Then she tried architecture, designing the family home in New South Wales. Next came romance writing—"the hardest and most challenging of all the activities," she confesses.

Books by Emma Darcy

Don't miss any of our special offers. Write to us at the following address for information on our newest releases.

Harlequin Reader Service
901 Fuhrmann Blvd., P.O. Box 1397, Buffalo, NY 14240
Canadian address: P.O. Box 603,
Fort Erie, Ont. L2A 5X3

EMMA DARCY

don't ask me now

Harlequin Books

TORONTO • NEW YORK • LONDON
AMSTERDAM • PARIS • SYDNEY • HAMBURG
STOCKHOLM • ATHENS • TOKYO • MILAN

Harlequin Presents first edition June 1987
ISBN 0-373-10984-9

Original hardcover edition published in 1986
by Mills & Boon Limited

CHAPTER ONE

THE customer shook his head in pleasurable incredulity. 'Amazing. Precisely what I'm looking for. Where did you get it?'

Cathy smiled a quiet triumph. Tom had also shaken his head over this particular piece, doubting its saleability, but her judgement seemed about to be vindicated. 'It's actually a draper's table. It came from an old general store in Wauchope, a timber town on the North Coast.'

'Yes, I know it. On the Hastings River,' the customer nodded. 'A draper's table?' he added quizzically.

'For displaying and cutting up bolts of cloth. That's why it's so long and wide. The drawers were used to store scissors, pins, cotton reels, ribbons, laces, buttons; all the paraphernalia for sewing. There was a brass rule inlaid along the edge for measuring out material, but it had to be removed when I had the surface levelled. I've kept it should the purchaser wish to have it relaid.'

'No.' Again he shook his head. 'It's the perfect size for storing and displaying my charts. And solid cedar, you say?'

'Absolutely.' Cathy slid out a couple of drawers to show him the rich, red-brown grain of the wood.

'Ah, they don't make drawers like that these days. All glued, you know. Just look at those beautiful

5

joins! Real workmanship.'

'That's one of the reasons why antiques command the price they do,' Cathy warned gently.

The man had never been in her shop before or she would have remembered him. Cathy never forgot a face. Many people admired and coveted antiques and were drawn into fantasising ownership, but they did not have the means to buy. This man was well past fifty and while his clothes were of good quality, they were well worn and slightly shabby. He had not taken her hint to ask for the price. He was still opening drawers, checking that they ran smoothly.

A quick glance at her watch showed that it was already ten minutes past the time she had planned to leave. Normally Cathy put any would-be customer ahead of all other considerations, but tonight ... toniqht was very important to her. It did not matter how many times she told herself it shouldn't be. It was. No amount of steely will-power could rationalise away the emotional wounds of the past and not even four years of achievement had healed them. Maybe, after tonight, she could finally put the past aside.

Cathy almost jumped at the light tap on her shoulder. Annoyed with her own inner tension she inadvertently frowned at her assistant. Barbara offered an apologetic smile and whispered her message.

'Mr Crawford's in the office. He says he wants to see you immediately and I'm to take over the customer.'

Cathy's frown disappeared, and an ironic smile took its place. Tom was making sure she left the shop in plenty of time. She glanced up to the office which was half a floor above the showroom. Tom's large, solid frame loomed behind the glass panel. His beetling eyebrows were lowered in disapproval and his unruly brown hair looked as if he had raked impatient fingers through it. He appeared formidable but Cathy knew that a kind, caring heart beat in that massive chest.

He was neither tall nor handsome. His features were too strong and heavy, particularly the Roman nose and the squarish jaw set on a short, thick neck. But the strength of character stamped on his face and apparent in the sharply intelligent brown eyes more than compensated for any lack of physical beauty. He was attractive to Cathy; too attractive for her peace of mind, because he was beyond her reach.

She turned to the customer and touched his arm lightly to gain his attention. 'I'm sorry, Mr . . .'

'Henleigh—Ralph Henleigh,' he supplied automatically.

She smiled. 'My name is Cathy Lawrence, Mr Henleigh. I have a call from my business partner. My assistant here, Barbara Unwin, will do all she can to help you. Mr Henleigh is interested in this table for his charts, Barbara.'

'Charts, Mr Henleigh? Are you a geographer?' Barbara suggested brightly.

The customer chuckled appreciation of her interest. 'No, young lady, a historian. And . . .'

Cathy beat a discreet retreat, feeling a very satisfying confidence in her assistant. Barbara was good at the job. She had soaked up everything Cathy had taught her, even to fixing customers' names in her mind by the simple method of repetition. Whatever business could be done this evening was safely left in Barbara's capable hands. Whether Cathy herself could get through this evening successfully was a question she couldn't answer.

Tom need not have come to check on her, but where she was concerned he had a tendency to double-check everything. She knew he did not understand her reservations. She also knew he was intent on overcoming them. But not even all the wealth and status of Thomas Henry Crawford the Third could help her if she was wrong tonight. The old sense of inferiority clutched at her heart as she opened the door into her office.

Tom gave her a crooked smile which mixed exasperation with his pleasure at seeing her. 'You are past the point of having to oversee every transaction personally, you know.'

'Tom, it's good business,' she insisted glibly, hiding her unease as she moved to the desk to pick up her handbag.

He heaved a sigh and lifted her jacket from the back of the chair. 'There's more to life than doing good business, Cathy.'

She flashed a smile over her shoulder at him as she slid her arms into the jacket he held for her. 'Now where would I have got with that attitude? I'd still owe you money, Tom.'

He swung her around, his hands resting lightly on her waist. The sudden softness on her face and the warm glow in the brown eyes sent a jangling warning along Cathy's nerves.

'But the money was never important to me, Cathy.'

Her teeth gritted. Of course money wasn't important to those who had plenty of it. 'It was to me,' she said tightly.

'You made it an unnecessary barrier between us for years,' he argued, and his voice gathered a deeper conviction as he added, 'And as for tonight, I want you to know that nothing is more important to me than having you at my side.'

Tears pricked at her eyes and she fought them with anger. It was easy for Tom to say that. It could even be true. But Tom was born and bred to the top levels of society. It was in his blood, in his nature. Cathy knew all too well what it was like to be an outsider. She forced a brittle smile. 'Well, I'd better get myself home and make myself beautiful for you.'

He forestalled her move away from him, sliding his hands around her back and pulling her into a gentle embrace. 'You don't have to make yourself beautiful. You already are.'

He wanted to kiss her. Cathy couldn't cope with it, not with tonight looming over her. She wouldn't be able to respond. Her hands pressed a quick protest against his powerful shoulders. 'Not here, Tom. You know I don't like public shows of affection,' she gabbled breathlessly.

'This isn't exactly public,' he retorted drily.

She nodded towards the glass panel. 'Nor is it completely private.'

'Cathy . . .' For a moment it seemed that her tension had been transmitted to him. Then he sighed and took her elbow to steer her out of the office.

She was intensely grateful to Tom for his
forbearance. She doubted that many men would put
up with the restraints she had placed on their
relationship and she knew she was trying him to the
limit. Sometimes she hated the barriers she felt
forced to keep between them. But self-preservation
was her strongest instinct, and despite her deep
affection for him, Tom belonged to the same class of
society as the man who had almost destroyed her,
and that she could never forget. Maybe if she was
accepted tonight, if she could fit in without raising
any eyebrows . . .

Barbara gave Cathy a gleeful sale-in-the-bag sign
as she and Tom walked through the shop. So Mr
Henleigh had been a genuine buyer. It was always so
difficult to judge. She had made sales to the most
unlikely-looking buyers over the years, which just
went to prove the old adage, never judge on
appearances. Except in society, Cathy thought
grimly.

At least the business was safe. Tom was right
about that. Cathy no longer felt the threat of
bankruptcy just around the corner if she put a foot
wrong. Not that Tom would ever have let that
happen to her, she realised now, but she had made it
on her own. Six months ago she had paid back the
last instalment of the loan he had advanced her. She
was now a fully fledged partner with him in this
antique business, and with the discharge of the debt
had come the release of the financial barrier between
them.

But the social one was still very much in existence,
at least in Cathy's mind. Tom had kept to her world

up until this invitation. Now he wanted her to enter his. She had refused at first, categorically and so emotionally that Tom had been taken aback by her reaction. He had slowly and calmly challenged every argument she had used, and in the end she knew she had to face it: either that or lose Tom. Though she would probably lose him anyway.

He escorted her to her car, waited as she unlocked it and handed her into the driver's seat. 'Eight o'clock,' he reminded her. 'And I promise you it'll be all right.' He shut the door, smiled reassurance, and stepped back to wave her off.

She hoped it would be all right. Over the four years she had been in Sydney, Cathy had absorbed and practised all the superficial trappings of a cultured sophisticate. Her speech was impeccable, her clothes-sense beyond criticism, her manners irreproachable. She knew all the finer points of etiquette. But inside the polished shell of Cathy Lawrence was a sense of worth which had been crushed to nothingness, and despite the rebuilding and the steady achievements of years, she was afraid of tonight, afraid of the world Tom had been born to, afraid to be found wanting, as she had been found wanting five years ago.

And the fear grew. It glazed her eyes as she stared unseeingly at her reflection in the mirror when she was finally ready. It stiffened her smile when Tom poured out effusive compliments about her appearance. It strangled all her replies to his conversation on the trip into the city. It turned her knees to jelly as Tom escorted her to the ballroom. Cinderella about to be unmasked, she thought despairingly, while they waited to be greeted by the official reception committee. The support of Tom's arm was of little consolation to her.

The party ahead of them moved off into the ballroom proper. Tom nudged her forward. Cathy tensed as Vera Pallister's eyes swept her from head to foot in sharp appraisal. This was the acid test. If the generally acknowledged queen of Sydney society gave her the nod of approval, then Cathy had a good chance of making it through the night. Every extravagant cent she had spent on her ball-gown would be worthwhile, even if she never wore the dress again.

Her heart was pumping so hard, she wondered if the wild palpitation could be seen under the ribbed silk jersey which hugged her figure like a second skin. She held her breath. The low-cut neckline swooped down to the soft swell of her breasts and Cathy did not want to reveal any agitation.

She briefly wondered if she should have chosen a more discreet style, but vanity had swayed her decision. She had the taut slimness and the right proportion of curves to carry off the svelte line of the dress. Besides, the frothy, petalled sleeves and the gored panels of chiffon petals in the lower skirt softened the sexy effect.

Cathy was sure she could not be found wanting on her use of make-up. It was a masterpiece of understatement. Her training as a cosmetician in those long-ago teenage years had taught her the skills she had applied too freely in the old days. She knew better now. The white dress had demanded the utmost subtlety. The only obvious colouring on her face was the rose-pink lipstick and the suggestion of turquoise shading above her blue eyes.

The testing eye of the shrewd society arbiter lingered on Cathy's hair-style. Her thick black hair had been cut and shaped by Marc Eamens himself, the top-line hairdresser of the fashion scene. Cathy had rejected the extreme frizz favoured by some fashion models, but had been persuaded into a more subdued version of the style. The fine, regular features of her oval face were now framed by a bouncing halo of soft, shiny curls, a dreamy effect of utter femininity.

A twitch of appreciation curved Vera Pallister's mouth as her gaze turned to the man at Cathy's side. Sharp appraisal softened into welcoming pleasure. 'Nice to see you, Tom. And so beautifully accompanied.' One carefully arched eyebrow rose questioningly.

'Miss Cathy Lawrence, Mrs Vera Pallister,' Tom reeled off with a touch of amused pride.

'Lawrence?'

Inwardly Cathy bristled at the note of snobbery in the question, but she stretched her lips in a confident smile. 'You wouldn't know my family, Mrs Pallister. They're country people.'

'Cathy's a business associate of mine,' Tom added with more pronounced pride.

'Indeed?' Interest sharpened the silky voice. 'And what business is that, my dear?'

'Antique furniture. Buying and selling,' Cathy answered briefly.

'Another good investment, Tom?' The question had a touch of indulgence.

Tom grinned, his soft brown eyes twinkling at Cathy. 'The best I've ever made.'

Vera laughed and patted his hand. 'Give my regards to your mother next time you see her.' She smiled warmly at Cathy. 'I hope you both enjoy the ball.'

Elation danced through Cathy's veins as Tom steered her away from the reception committee. She had passed. She had been accepted. She was here at the most prestigious event of the social calendar, *the* charity ball of the year, and even Vera Pallister had welcomed her. Maybe it really was possible for the last barrier to be set aside.

'Mr Crawford, a moment please.'

A photographer was beckoning an invitation to pose beside a marble pedestal which held a magnificent arrangement of flowers.

Tom hesitated, then smiled at Cathy. 'Why not? I'd like a picture of you in that dress.'

They posed. The camera clicked. A society reporter took note. 'The lady's name, Mr Crawford?'

'Miss Cathy Lawrence. The owner of The Cedar Heritage. Best antiques in Sydney,' Tom rattled off like a publicity agent.

Cathy dug her elbow in his ribs as he led her away. 'I thought tonight was supposed to be strictly pleasure.'

'Never look down your nose at a business plug in the society pages,' he retorted archly. 'The women who read them are all potential customers.'

She laughed. 'They won't put me in the society pages!'

'Of course they will. The caption will read "The

most beautiful woman at the ball".'

'More likely "On the arm of Thomas Henry Crawford, the Third",' she mocked, but her inner exhilaration sparkled in her voice. She had been photographed for the society pages. Even if the photograph was not used, she had been seen as worthy of note, a woman of class. She hugged Tom's arm in an access of happiness and gratitude. She could not have done it without his support and encouragement.

His answering smile brought a warm glow to her heart. He was not usually a smiling person, but when his face did relax into lines of pleasure he seemed extraordinarily attractive. With his brown eyes twinkling at her, his unruly hair tidily groomed and his stocky body looking impressively masculine in the formal tailoring of a dinner-suit, he looked very handsome indeed to Cathy. And she was enormously pleased that to him she was the most beautiful woman at the ball.

The orchestra was not playing as they entered the ballroom, and Cathy was conscious of eyes turning their way as an usher escorted them to their table. She pretended not to notice, walking with unhurried grace and dignity, confident now that her appearance was above snobbish criticism. It was a marvellous feeling.

Nervous tension attacked her again as Tom introduced her to his friends at the table. She would be spending the night with these people and she would need more than appearance to carry her through. She concentrated on remembering all their names. As each introduction took place she chanted

the name to herself while she smiled and looked
intensely at the person. It was a habit that she had
developed soon after going into business for herself,
and her good memory had impressed many customers. The women regarded her with interest and
curiosity, the men with admiration, and Cathy found
herself being accepted amongst them with an ease
which amazed and excited her.

The orchestra started up a bracket of slow
numbers. The dance-floor was quickly populated,
and Cathy drank in the whole fascinating scene with
avid eyes. Never had she seen such an ostentatious
display of wealthy dressing. Some of the ball-gowns
were absolutely stunning and drew knowing comments from the other women at the table.

'So that's this year's Yves St Laurent!'

'Mmmh. I like Joscelyn's better—it's a Karl
Lagerfeld from Chanel.'

'Doesn't do much for her. Give me Valentino, or
Gianfranco Ferre. He always has marvellous subtlety of line. Just look at Felicity Fanshaw. She looks
fabulous!'

'Well, Vera Pallister's given the snub to European
designers this year. Gone to the Americans. Word is
that she's wearing a Geoffrey Beene.'

'I don't know why anyone bothers going past the
Australian designers. I love your dress, Cathy. It's a
Prue Acton, isn't it?'

'Thank you,' Cathy smiled, ignoring the question.
She had learnt the art of letting people draw their
own conclusions. Better to say too little than too
much. Besides, she had no interest in competing with
other women. She just wanted to luxuriate in the

sense of belonging.

'Would you like to dance?' Tom murmured in her ear.

'Love to,' she breathed happily.

He pushed his chair back from the table, rose to his feet and helped her to hers. He was not a tall man, only just topping Cathy's above-average height, but he was immensely strong, stronger than any man Cathy had ever known. His shoulders and arms were thickly muscled and the breadth of his chest was such that she felt fragile and feminine when he took her in his arms, particularly since Tom invariably held her as if she might break unless he was careful. Nevertheless, despite his stolid frame he was a good dancer, moving lightly and accurately to the music.

'Is it a Prue Acton?' he asked, eyes twinkling with amusement.

She laughed and shook her head. 'I don't know what it is. I simply liked the dress, so I bought it.'

He smiled. 'It does you justice. Women can be terrible cats when it comes to clothes. God knows why—it's the person who should count.'

'I'm glad you think so, Tom. I'd never have climbed off the ground without your belief in me.'

'Nonsense. You had the drive and the ambition to make it, and I was lucky enough to recognise your particular stamp of quality. If it hadn't been me, there would have heen someone else. There always is at the beginning of any venture.'

'No, it wasn't just financial backing.' He had been supportive, encouraging and helpful, but more than that, he had given her respect, and now he had brought her here and proved that she could win anyone's respect. Her eyes shone with the fulfilment of an impossible dream as she added, 'You made me feel as if I were your equal. Even then, when I was little more than a beggar on your doorstep.'

The bemused look on his face told her that he didn't understand. A person of Tom's social background would never completely understand, but that didn't matter any more. Cathy had been accepted, seen as 'one of them', and readily included in their company.

'Cathy, no one would ever have considered you a beggar. You had your business proposition thought out to the last decimal point. One of the most lucid and comprehensive propositions I've ever had put to me.'

She grinned, too happy to argue with him, too happy to recall the tight desperation and fierce determination which had forced her to their first meeting in the office of Thomas Crawford Investments. That was all in the past. Four years in the past. Five years if she counted from the time her decision had been made. Five years of hard slog, five years of risking everything on her own judgement and a burning will to lift herself to better things. Five years that had finally paid off, with Tom's help.

Exhilaration prompted an uncharacteristic impulse. She pressed closer to Tom and kissed his cheek. 'Thank you for everything you've been to me,' she whispered.

His arms tightened around her. She felt his chest heave and the soft whistle of his breath through her hair as he leaned his head against hers. 'I've been rewarded, knowing you, being associated with you.

You've always delighted me.'

It was a lovely thing to say. But then Tom invariably said what Cathy wanted to hear. He was a wonderful person, the best friend she could ever have hoped to have, and maybe now she could let him be more than a friend. Her heart swelled with feeling for him and her sigh was one of happy relief, of a burden being laid aside.

Tom deftly manoeuvred her to the centre of the dance-floor where there was less crowding, and Cathy's exultant sense of being on the inside of this very exclusive world was heightened even further. Her eyes sparkled over the dancers whirling around her, enjoying every bit of glitter and high-spirited gaiety, until her gaze caught the sun-bleached hair, half a head above the crowd.

A sickening jolt hit her stomach. It wasn't him! It couldn't be him, her mind argued frantically, fighting the shock which was still pummelling her stomach. In fascinated horror she watched the yellow-blond head moving closer. Purposefully closer? Dear God, please don't let it be him, Cathy prayed wildly.

CHAPTER TWO

THE bright yellow head did not veer away, it was coming straight towards her. Cathy's heart hammered alarm. She didn't want to see him, she never wanted to meet him again. Her life was just the way she wanted it now, better than she had ever dreamed possible. She wanted no reminders of the past, especially not him. Revulsion crawled down her spine. Especially not him. Never again was she going to suffer the humiliation of condescension, not from anyone.

But the bright-coloured hair kept moving closer, a magnet from which she could not tear her eyes. The dancers in between suddenly moved aside, allowing a moment of full-face confrontation. Green eyes bored into Cathy's, igniting memories which should have been dead and buried, but to her utter mortification, just that one brief look stirred a chaotic response.

Anthony! Her pulse beat out the name in an ever-quickening tempo, even after the gap had closed and only the top of his head was visible. Anthony! A trembling weakness started creeping through Cathy's body, frightening her into panic. Five years ... five years, she recited in a frantic grab for rationality. He shouldn't have this effect on her, not after all this time.

Then in wild contradiction to any common sense

came a fierce wave of exultation. Yes, let him come closer! Let him see her now, the woman who was once the girl his parents had judged not good enough for their son. And with almost primitive savagery, Cathy hoped he would regret the decision he had made. She was good enough for anyone tonight. No one here had found her wanting in any way.

Pride put a mask of composure over her inner turmoil. Anthony steered his partner to within reaching distance. Cathy's heart lost all sense of timing but pride met the question in the green eyes and pride curved her mouth into an amused little smile.

He recognised her all right, but recognition was fighting a battle with incredulity. She could see no change in him, except for a slight deepening of lines about the eyes, stunning eyes in a darkly tanned, handsome face. Every girl in Armidale had envied Anthony's attention to her. His clean-cut good looks, his outstanding physique and a natural charm of manner had made him the most desirable catch in town. Only Anthony was not catchable material for a girl of Cathy's background.

His partner made some remark. He gave distracted acknowledgement to it but his attention barely moved from Cathy. He frowned as his gaze drifted over her hair. Long hair it had been then, a black curtain of rippling waves, falling to below her shoulder-blades, untouched by any hairdresser. His eyes traced the lines of her face, more delicately defined with a significant loss of weight, down the graceful length of her throat to the hollows which he had kissed so many times, passionately, murmuring words of love.

Cathy felt the flush of heat creeping into her cheeks and could do nothing to stop it. A wave of shame made her turn her face away. She couldn't really care about Anthony now. She was with Tom, the man who had given her the faith that Anthony had lacked. There was a solid comfort and security in Tom's arms that she had never experienced in Anthony's.

With Anthony it had been a feverish obsession, climbing turbulent heights and plumbing the depths of despair; a tormenting love which ultimately gave more pain than pleasure. In the end he hadn't wanted her enough, and that she could never forget. So let it go, she told herself sternly, sensibly. Anthony was the past, a different life ago.

The dance ended. Cathy determinedly used Tom as a block against Anthony, hanging on his arm and talking animatedly as they wove their way back to the table. Shock had momentarily knocked her off balance but the shock was over now. She was not going to let anything or anyone spoil this night for her.

She settled back in her chair and consciously relaxed. She enjoyed listening to the chatter of the other women, privately amused by the status-conscious trivia of their socialite lives. Tom poured her a glass of champagne. The steady warmth in his eyes soothed her into complacency. A waiter placed a huge platter of hors d'oeuvres on the table, and she took a crouton spread with pâté and sprinkled with caviare and found it delicious. She picked up another to hand to Tom.

'You'll like this,' she declared, turning to him with an encouraging smile, and almost dropped it in his lap as she saw Anthony making straight for their table.

Tom took the bite-piece, popped it into his mouth and nodded towards the approaching figure. 'Someone you know?'

'Yes,' she breathed, tautened nerves strangling her voice. She swallowed hard to beat the constriction in her throat and picked up her glass of champagne in a forced pose of unconcern.

'Cathy.' The deep, resonant voice she remembered so well sent vibrations right down to her toes.

'Hello, Anthony. I didn't expect to see you here,' she said coolly, an ocean of reserve in the blue eyes which held his with determined steadiness.

He was watching for any tell-tale flicker of reaction. 'Nor I you,' he answered softly before turning to Tom and offering his hand. 'Anthony Pryor-Jones. I understand you know my sister Vanessa.'

'Ah, yes,' Tom replied brightly, taking the hand as he rose to his feet. 'She's here, is she?'

Anthony nodded in the direction of his table. 'You must come over later and say hello. Van was just saying she hadn't seen you for ages.'

Tom gave a non-committal smile and offered introductions, but Anthony already knew most of the people in their party. Cathy bitterly berated herself for blind stupidity as polite small-talk was exchanged. Didn't she know that the very wealthy all belonged to the same charmed circle? They went to the same exclusive schools, the same social occasions, the same charity balls.

How could she have been so short-sighted as not to have considered that Anthony might be here tonight? Distance meant nothing to a family that owned a private plane, and the Pryor-Jones family of Mirrima would have to be at the top of the social register in New South Wales, if not all of Australia. Top of the landed gentry anyway. No one who had ever seen the property of Mirrima could doubt it.

Mirrima, that cruel, fabulous jewel of a property which had crushed Cathy's hope of marrying Anthony even before his parents had opened fire on her. Her chest constricted at the thought of seeing Stephanie and Carlton Pryor-Jones again. Were they here too? Anthony had only mentioned Vanessa. Well, so what if they were here, Cathy told herself belligerently. She had been good enough for Vera Pallister, good enough for Tom's friends, good enough for Tom.

It was surely curiosity that had drawn Anthony to her table. It could not really be anything else, not after five years. But curiosity meant he would be asking her questions. Cathy encased herself in hard, protective walls, anticipating some telling reference to the past. The mental toughness she had learnt over the last few years was sharpened to readiness. Let Anthony say what he liked, she silently challenged, and he would not be met with a meek, defeatist reply.

He turned to Tom with the charming smile which used to twist her heart. 'I must confess it was your partner who drew me over here. Do you mind if I

talk to Cathy for a while? Haven't seen her for years.'
The smile shone on her. 'We've a lot to catch up on.'

'Be our guest,' Tom invited affably. 'Though I
can't guarantee that the chair next to Cathy will
remain vacant for long. But until Fiona returns . . .'

'Kind of you,' Anthony tossed off pleasantly as he
took up the invitation.

He leant his hand on the back of Cathy's chair as
he moved in behind her and left his arm resting there
when he sat down. Cathy stiffened forward, instinctively avoiding his touch while every nerve tingled
awareness of the man she had known so intimately.
Tom resumed his seat and impulsively she reached
for his hand, linking herself to him in a blind need to
ward off the past that Anthony embodied all too
disturbingly.

'Are you living in Sydney now?' The sparkling
interest in his voice spelt danger to Cathy.

'Yes. I moved down some years ago,' she answered
matter-of-factly.

He shook his head, a whimsical smile on his lips.
'Funny, I've thought of you as settled in Armidale,
married . . . a couple of kids.'

'You knew Cathy in Armidale?' Tom asked
curiously. Cathy held her breath, willing Anthony to
be discreet.

'Yes. I did an agricultural science course at the
university there,' he replied smoothly. 'Cathy was
very much a hometown girl in those days. I'm
astonished to find her here.'

Tom laughed. 'Open his eyes some more, Cathy.
Tell him you're the best businesswoman in Sydney.'

'Business?'

'Tom is in the habit of singing my praises,' she said drily. 'It's his way of protecting his percentage.' She actually enjoyed Anthony's puzzlement.

'What business?'

'Old furniture.' Cathy's smile mocked the incredulity in his eyes. 'It was your mother who pointed out the value of antiques to me, Anthony. You can thank her for me. I owe her for that, and for a great many other things.'

His eyes narrowed thoughtfully and he spoke with a slow deliberation. 'You've certainly come a long way.'

'Yes, a long way,' she agreed curtly. 'And what about you? Are you married with a couple of kids?'

The twist of his lips acknowledged the edge of irony. 'No, much to my parents' discontent. Is everything well with your family?'

'As far as I know.'

She could sense Tom's puzzlement in the short silence which followed her clipped reply. She had never spoken of her family to Tom, in fact, she had brushed off any enquiry about her previous life in Armidale.

'No reconciliation, Cathy?' came Anthony's soft murmur. As if he cared!

Cathy gritted her teeth. He hadn't cared, not then. He had been pleased to have her free of her family. It had not mattered to him that her father had called her a lusting whore and thrown her out of the only home she had known.

'Some things don't change,' she said flippantly, then breathed a sigh of relief as she spotted Fiona making her way back to the table. A few more moments and this ordeal would be over.

The orchestra started up again. Anthony climbed to his feet. 'All right if I have this dance with Cathy, Tom?'

No! she screamed silently.

'That's up to Cathy,' said Tom with a slight suggestion of reluctance.

She rushed in. 'I don't think . . .'

'Oh, come on, we used to do it so well. For old times' sake, Cathy.'

She was caught. A refusal would be boorish after such an exchange of familiarity, there could be no reasonable excuse for it. As it was, Tom's curiosity was aroused. Anthony was obviously prepared to arouse it further if she did not fall in with his wishes.

Damn him! she cursed silently. Why couldn't he have left her alone, as he had done so ruthlessly when she had needed him most? Her only consolation was that by dancing with him, she could speak her mind without Tom's overhearing things she did not want him to know. Her past was her own private affair, nothing to do with the life she had made for herself in Sydney.

She stood up and flashed a smile at Tom, who gave a dismissive shrug which seemed to roll disappointment into resignation. She squeezed his shoulder affectionately as she passed behind him and he turned a smile of pleasure towards her. Some of her inner tension eased, but her body stiffened with resentment when Anthony pulled her against him.

'Are you frightened of me, Cathy?' he murmured close to her ear.

'No,' she denied swiftly.

'Then why don't you relax?'

She forced herself to relax. It was a mistake. Anthony's hand ran down the curve of her spine, pressing her even closer, awakening memories which could not be shrugged aside.

'Why did you turn away from me?'

The low, intense whisper threw her into confusion.

It was he who had turned away from her. Unless he meant tonight when she had been dancing with Tom.

'What's the point, Anthony?' she demanded, her voice tight and strained. 'It was over between us long ago.'

'It wasn't over, not for me. It never was for me. That last night when you turned away from me, I thought you'd found another man. What else could I think? It'd been almost two months since we'd been together and you didn't want to make love. You were distant and unresponsive all evening. There had to be another man, so who was he? Why didn't he marry you?'

He sucked in a sharp breath and his voice throbbed with emotion as he added, 'It ripped my guts out saying goodbye to you that night. You were my first love, and my only love. And I'll be damned if I'll walk away now!'

CHAPTER THREE

PAIN wrenched her heart. Reason fought it. Anthony had to be lying, it hadn't been like that. He was twisting the truth which damned him as the inconstant lover. The distance had been in his eyes that last night. Judgement had been passed by his parents and accepted by him. Cathy Lawrence was not good enough for Anthony Pryor-Jones.

It had been in his over-bright voice at the dinner they had attended with his family. It had been in his need to gather others around them at the Graduation Ball. It had been in his carefully casual enquiry if she was still safe against pregnancy when he drove her to his motel. His irritable acceptance of her decision not to make love with him had confirmed it even further. He had made no attempt at persuasion, no talk of next time. And finally, it had been in his hurry to leave once he had delivered her to her door.

Cathy had needed no further underlining, and words would have piled hurt on top of hurt which had been close to unbearable. The last tatter of pride had carried her through that night. The situation had been so painfully clear to her. An arrangement had been made, and honour demanded that it be kept. But that had been the predetermined cut-off line to an affair which should never have been entered into at all.

A surge of bitterness sharpened her voice. 'You

know there was no other man. Don't take me for a fool, Anthony. You were giving me the kiss-off that night.' She raised hard, mocking eyes to his. 'Do you really think I didn't know?'

He feigned bewilderment. 'The what?'

Anger blistered her reply. 'You know damned well you had no intention of keeping our relationship going! I wasn't a suitable wife for a Pryor-Jones.'

'Did I ever say that? Did I?' he demanded vehemently.

'You didn't have to,' she shot back at him, eyes flashing the depth of her resentment for what had been done to her. 'Don't pretend you weren't aware of what was going on that fortnight I spent with your family. You heard most of the subtle little put-downs which showed me up as an inferior species. I hadn't gone to the right schools, I wore too much make-up, my clothes were all wrong, I was ignorant of all the little niceties of high society. And that weird religion my family was caught up in . . . my dear, how very difficult for you!' she mimicked savagely.

'They didn't matter,' Anthony grated harshly. 'None of those things mattered to me. You know why I haven't married? Because after you, no other woman measured up.'

'The only place I measured up was in bed, Anthony. Why don't you just admit it? It's all so long ago.'

'No! It's now!'

The intense passion in his voice shook her. She was shaken even further when he thrust her body against his and hard muscle met her soft flesh.

'Just the sight of you arouses desire in me. Holding

you like this...Cathy, I want you!' His thighs
pushed hers into a sequence of dance-steps which
provoked a nerve-shattering rush of memories. His
mouth whispered across her hair. 'You're responding to me, Cathy. It's not over. It's the same as it
always was with us.'

'No,' she choked out, fighting the seduction of his
words even though her body was tingling with
traitorous heat. 'Stop it, Anthony!'

'You used to like dancing with me like this, teasing
me with your body, anticipation sparkling in your
eyes, the flush of excitement on your cheeks. They're
flushing now, Cathy.'

She hated herself for being so affected by him, and
hated him for making her feel so vulnerable to his
physical magnetism. 'If you don't stop this I swear
I'll kick you, Anthony!'

He loosened his hold, but the green eyes were
glinting with triumph. 'Just proving that it's still
there for us, Cathy.'

She drew in a deep breath, trying to calm her
leaping pulse-rate. Her whole wretched body was out
of control, but her mind fought to grasp essentials.
'You might still want me, Anthony, but don't tell me
it's love. It never was love, or you wouldn't have let
your parents win.'

His jaw tightened. 'You let them win, Cathy. They
hammered me with a thousand arguments between
the time you left our home and the Graduation
weekend. We were both too young, you were this and
that, and I hadn't met enough girls to be making a
lifelong choice. Oh, it went on week after week, but I
came to you, didn't I? I kept faith with you. It was

you who backed off. Don't say I didn't love you. I loved you,' he repeated vehemently.

The glittering passion in the green eyes was so strong, so convincing, that Cathy was lost to all rational thought. The love she had given to this man was a live, pulsing tidal wave of memories, sweeping five years into forgettable flotsam. Maybe he hadn't faltered in his love for her. Maybe his parents had manipulated them both that night. But he could have spoken, made his feelings clear, not just left her with that soul-destroying silence. Cathy shook her head in helpless confusion, not knowing what to believe.

He tugged at her heart again, increasing her emotional turmoil. 'It can be different for us now, Cathy. When I saw you here tonight ... God! I couldn't describe the sheer torrent of feeling which shot through me. I wish my parents were here to see you. They'd be forced to eat every damnable word they spoke against you. We can make another start, Cathy.'

'No!' The cry broke from her lips, an instinctive and instant reaction to a time of such torment she couldn't bear any part of it to be repeated. She enjoyed a good life now, interesting, challenging, and fulfilling. She was happy with Tom. It had taken too long to establish what she had for her to risk Anthony's disturbing it all. And he would, she knew he would. Let the past stay in the past, she determined with panicky resolution. 'I like my relationship with Tom,' she stated in tight defence.

The green eyes probed in a relentless quest for the vulnerability she was hiding. 'Are you living with him?'

Heat rushed into her cheeks, angry, proud heat. 'No, I'm not. I make my own living, just as I've always done.'

'Then you don't feel for him what you felt for me. You can turn your back on what we had, Cathy. You did it before, and no doubt you can do it again. But it was something so special between us, I can't believe you'll ever find it with anyone else. I know I haven't.'

She didn't know if that was true. She could not compare what she had with Tom with what had been between her and Anthony. It was too different, two entirely different backgrounds, two different lives.

Anthony's hand slid caressingly to the nape of her neck. Fingers began a gentle stroking which stirred ripples of pleasure under her skin. 'Cathy.' He breathed the name with a husky longing which found a painful echo in her own heart. 'Give it a chance.'

'No, I don't want it. I don't want it,' she repeated in agitated protest at what he was doing to her, and what he might do to her if she gave him the chance.

'No two people in the whole world have loved so totally as we did. But if it would make you happier to walk away from me now, then do it. Because all I want is to make you happy.'

Anthony stopped dancing. His hands slid down to hers, a fingertip grasp which held her there more strongly than any embrace. The choice was hers. She could walk away now. But did she really want to? What if he had been speaking the truth? Oh how he could twist her around so much. But she had given herself to him totally, with destructive totality.

'Do you love Tom?'

Her emotions were in such a state of churning conflict that she couldn't find an answer. 'I don't know. I don't know what I feel,' she moaned despairingly.

Anthony gently pulled her into his arms, holding her with a tenderness which made her tremble. It was suddenly very close, that blind, all-consuming love which had almost destroyed her.

'You did love me once, Cathy.'

She had loved him so much she had given up everything for him . . . her family, her religion, her whole way of life. But she could not, would not take that path again. The cost was too high if Anthony let her down as he had last time. Or had he? She wasn't sure of anything any more, except that he could still draw a strong response from her, a response so strong that all her judgements were crashing around her.

The music stopped. There was a general movement towards tables and the crowd of dancers quickly thinned.

Anthony's eyes burnt into hers, scorching a path to her heart. 'Don't leave me now,' he murmured huskily, then hugged her to his side, a possessive arm around her waist as he began walking her off the dance-floor.

Cathy's confusion of mind was so great that she did not notice the direction he had chosen. When it finally registered she stopped dead. 'I can't go with you. I can't leave Tom at our table. I must go back,' she said distractedly.

For a moment it seemed as if Anthony would challenge her, but his eyes softened to the agitated appeal in hers. 'All right. We'll go and get Tom and bring him with us. He can talk to Vanessa.'

He was taking control. It had always been so with Anthony, a roller-coaster to happiness or despair. And now he intended to involve Tom with Vanessa so that he could keep her to himself. It wasn't fair. She couldn't allow Tom to be manipulated like an insignificant pawn, she owed him so much. Without him she would never have made it anywhere, let alone to this ball, and the very least he deserved was the courtesy of her full attention.

But Tom's attention was not on her as she and Anthony approached the table. A woman had taken Cathy's chair and drawn him into a huddle of private conversation. A surge of relief washed through Cathy. Tom would not have noticed anything amiss in her behaviour just now or during the dancing.

A silky fall of blonde hair hid the woman's features until Cathy and Anthony arrived at Tom's side, but there was no mistaking her identity then. Vanessa, Anthony's younger sister, was certainly no schoolgirl now. She looked the very epitome of a sophisticated beauty, shining with the polish of wealth.

The black taffeta ball-gown screamed couturier label and the aquamarine necklace was undoubtedly set in real diamonds. Her eyes were her most remarkable feature. Not as green as Anthony's, they had a bluish tinge which was almost aqua. They were alight with avid interest.

'Cathy! I couldn't believe it was you when you walked in with Tom,' she declared lightly. 'Even Anthony did a double-take. If I'd known you were in Sydney all this time, I would have looked you up.'

'That would have been nice, Vanessa,' Cathy replied just as lightly. Hot air, sweet nothing, that was all Vanessa's comment had been, she thought cynically. The two of them had about as much in common as a mink and a rabbit.

'Van's been living with our grandmother at Double Bay while she's supposed to be studying veterinary science at Sydney University. It takes her two years to pass one year's work,' Anthony supplied drily.

'Thanks!' Vanessa stood up in huffed protest. 'Just when I'm trying to impress on Tom that I'm not an idle emptyhead!'

Tom laughed and shook his head at her. 'I wouldn't, for one moment, consider you an empty-head, Vanessa.'

She leaned over and kissed his cheek in playful appreciation. 'You always say the right thing, Tom.'

She was right, he did. But Cathy was bemused by the ease of Vanessa'a little act of affection. She herself had done the same thing earlier tonight, but she could not have done it so lightly.

Tom smiled up at Cathy with a welcoming warmth which denied any fascination with Anthony's beautiful sister. Cathy's taut nerves relaxed a little with that reassurance. It surprised her to find herself feeling possessive about him, but Anthony had rocked her so badly she needed Tom's steady support to soothe her inner turbulence. He took her hand and she automatically returned the light pressure of his fingers.

Anthony tightened his hold on her waist and spoke with overriding charm. 'No need to break up the conversation with Tom, Van. I was just going to invite him and Cathy over to our table. Make it an old friends' reunion. Won't get another opportunity for a get-together for ages. We're flying back to Mirrima tomorrow, so let's make a night of it.'

Tom's quick frown sparked more persuasion.

'Oh, do come, Tom. It'll be fun,' urged Vanessa. 'We'll prove you're wrong about rural properties. Best investment there is.'

He pulled a rueful grimace. 'I was hoping to have Cathy to myself this evening.'

'What! A woman as beautiful and accomplished as Cathy!' Anthony gave a jocular laugh. 'You can't be so selfish, Tom. An hour or two of sharing won't hurt you.'

Tom cocked a questioning eyebrow at Cathy, and with an odd sense of inevitability she gave a little nod. Time to sort out her feelings, she told herself, but was discomfited about it. She owed Tom loyalty and any kind of deception was anathema to her. But she was not really deceiving him, she argued. She just needed time to assess the feelings Anthony had aroused.

Tom gracefully conceded defeat and Anthony took over as host, shepherding them to his table, procuring extra chairs, and making an exuberant play of the introductions to his party. They were all large property-owners from the north-west of the state, and Cathy was drily amused to hear Anthony put pointed emphasis on her birthplace.

'Cathy is one of us, country-bred, comes from Armidale. Tom needs to be converted. He thinks the

Stock-Exchange is an adequate substitute for wheat and sheep.'

'I'd take argument with you there, Anthony,' Tom commented smoothly. 'I don't need converting. The Crawford wealth was built on wheat and sheep. And we kept it by getting off the land at the right time,' he added with mischievous provocation.

He was howled down by the rest of the party and the ensuing conversation was lively, with Tom actively enjoying the controversy he kept stirring. Cathy was amazed to have her opinion lobbied for a general consensus against him, but loyalty dictated that she give Tom her support. Nevertheless she was unquestioningly accepted as 'one of them', and Cathy could not help thinking how ironic the situation was.

Here were Anthony and Vanessa projecting her as an equal and she had been treated as insignificant dirt under their parents' feet. Yet if Anthony had flouted his parents' wishes and married her, would these people have accepted her as readily as they had done tonight?

Her position was different now, because she was different. Anthony was right about that.

'Well, Tom, if you don't want to invest in land, you could always marry into it and have the best of both worlds,' Vanessa said flirtatiously.

'Now what man would want such a hard, unforgiving wife as the land? You're either flattened by a drought or a flood, not to mention bushfires, locusts, blight or blowflies. I think Job was a farmer, and God certainly put him through the trials of marriage with the land. Very wearing on a man,' he declared, eyes twinkling with devilment.

Cathy smiled. Tom was never short of a quick-witted reply. The banter rolled on, but Cathy's mind lingered on Vanessa's words. There was a truth in them that struck a chill warning. Land did marry land. Wealth married wealth. While she now had the *savoir-faire* to fit into this society she did not have the substance.

Jillian Barnsworth, the girl sitting on the other side of Anthony, undoubtedly did, and she was intent on staking a claim. Her hands couldn't leave Anthony alone and her eyes were devouring him. She only looked to be about eighteen, the same age as Cathy had been . . .

The old pain twisted her heart. Could she afford to let Anthony lay claim to her again? Was it worth the risk? Her eyes lifted to his and her uncertainty was met by an answering blaze of purpose before Anthony's gaze flicked to his sister.

'Let's show Tom what he's missing out on, Van. Ask him to come up to Mirrima for the weekend. He could fly home with us tomorrow.'

Vanessa clapped her hands with glee. 'Great idea! We've got you now, Tom. It's our yearly shindig this weekend. Everyone's flying or driving in from hundreds of kilometres around. The party just goes on and on. We'll test that city stamina to the limit with good old country fare.'

Tom laughed and leaned back in his chair, twinkling eyes turning to Cathy. 'Not for me, Vanessa, thanks all the same. I find all the excitement I want right here.'

'Can't let you off the hook,' Anthony persisted.

'Bring Cathy with you. It'll do you both good to have
a break from the city. Breathe clean, fresh air for a
change.' He turned to Cathy with an air of charming
concern. 'When was the last time you took a holiday,
Cathy?'

Oh no! Not Mirrima, Cathy thought in instant
recoil. She wouldn't go back there. 'Five years ago,'
she murmured, her eyes flashing a hard warning.

'Good God!' he exclaimed, and the challenge he
threw back at her was swiftly turned to Tom. 'What
kind of a friend would deprive her of a chance of
complete relaxation? Do the right thing, Tom. Insist
that she come with you.'

'I don't need a holiday, Anthony,' Cathy said
sharply. 'And I can't leave the business at weekends.'

'Nonsense! That statement just goes to show you
do need a rest. Come on, Tom—convince her.
Organise her. She must come with you.'

'Anthony's right, Cathy,' Tom suddenly agreed,
startling her with an eagerness which was in direct
contradiction to his earlier reluctance. 'Barbara's
perfectly capable of handling the business for one
weekend. Take the time off for once and come away
with me.'

He didn't know what he was asking, Cathy
thought in cringing dismay. To return to Mirrima
Homestead, with Anthony laying siege to her heart
and his parents looking askance at her? Tom would
be caught in the web Anthony was weaving as surely
as Cathy would be.

'Oh, do say yes, Cathy,' urged Vanessa. 'You can't
be a spoilsport!'

Cathy looked distractedly at her. Vanessa would

certainly not be standing on any sideline this time. She had her eye on Tom, or on Tom's wealth.

'Mirrima is at its best this time of year, there's no place like it. You'll get a warm welcome,' Anthony put in persuasively.

She flashed him a sceptical glance. Yet perhaps Mirrima was the place to sort out exactly what she felt about everything. It had staged the turning-point in her life five years ago. Maybe it would help provide the answers she needed now. With a strange sense of inevitability, of a wheel coming full circle and herself caught within that circle, she gave in. 'All right. I'll come.'

'Great!' Triumph rang in Anthony's voice. 'You'll both enjoy it, I promise.'

Tom was delighted, Vanessa was delighted, everyone was delighted. Cathy was a mass of seething fears, but she hid them behind a fac + acade of smiling pleasure.

'We'll be flying from Bankstown Airport at about two-thirty tomorrow afternoon. That suit you, Tom?' Anthony pressed.

'Fine,' he nodded. 'And I'll make sure Cathy gets there,' he added with a grin at her.

'That will give us time to recover from tonight and gets us home in plenty of time to relax before dinner,' said Anthony with anticipatory relish.

'Your parents won't mind a couple of extra guests landed on them?' Tom quizzed.

Vanessa laughed. 'Are you kidding? With two hundred or more people zooming in on us? This is hospitality weekend, open house.'

Hospitality, Cathy thought with grim irony. She

had tasted the hospitality of Carlton and Stephanie Pryor-Jones before and the taste was still bitter in her mouth. But she was no longer the naïve, ignorant girl on whom they had heaped their condescension. Carlton and Stephanie Pryor-Jones were in for a sharp surprise.

The thought gave her considerable satisfaction. If nothing else came of this weekend, she would prove something to herself in confronting Anthony's parents again.

CHAPTER FOUR

THE city was quiet. Tom's Mercedes hummed along almost empty streets. The tensions of the night gradually seeped out of Cathy's body, leaving her limp and tired. It was not so very late, only one o'clock. The ball was still in full swing, but she was glad Tom had suggested leaving. She had had enough.

If she was to be organised to her satisfaction for the weekend at Mirrima, she needed to be up early in the morning. It was not only the business which would need time and attention to detail, she had to fit in some shopping too. If she was going to Mirrima, she would go well prepared, no lamb to the slaughter this time.

'Will you need any help tomorrow?' asked Tom. 'I could lend a hand.'

She smiled at him, her eyes soft with affection and gratitude. He had always been ready to lend a helping hand. 'No, it'll be all right. I'm sure Barbara will cope very well.'

'It's a good thing, this weekend. You do need a break away from work.' He threw her a happy grin. 'And I'm going to enjoy being with you.'

Cathy could not imagine enjoying any part of a weekend at Mirrima, but she was glad that Tom would be with her. She knew she could count on his support. But what if she found herself drawn back to

Anthony? Tom would be hurt. She shot him a worried glance. The last thing in the world she wanted was to hurt Tom, and yet she could not push Anthony back into the past now. She had to find out the truth about his feelings, and her own.

'You've never told me about your family, Cathy,' Tom remarked on a softly enquiring note. 'I'd like to know.'

She hesitated for a long time before deciding there was no harm in satisfying a little of his curiosity. 'I was disowned by my family when I was seventeen,' she stated flatly. 'To them I don't exist any more.'

'Good God!' He turned appalled eyes to her. 'What happened?'

She sighed and closed her eyes. 'It's a different life ago, Tom. I don't want to remember it. I don't want to talk about it.'

He reached across and took her hand, squeezing it gently in silent comfort. It felt good to be linked to Tom. He had an innate strength which invariably bolstered her own. Again she began fretting over the uncertainties looming ahead.

'What about Anthony? Where does he fit in?'

Her heart jumped erratically and her eyes flew open to dart an agitated glance at Tom. His gaze was still on the road. He had asked the question quite casually. Cathy realised she should have been prepared for it. Natural curiosity would have prompted it after the events of the night. But she didn't know where Anthony fitted in. That was the question tormenting her. Still, she had to reply; tonight's familiarity needed some explanation.

'My first job was as a shop assistant in a

pharmacy. Anthony was a student at the university. He used to come into the shop to buy things, and we got to know each other pretty well. Then I went out with him for a while. I haven't seen him since he graduated from his course.'

So much pain hidden behind a few glib words, Cathy thought grimly. Tom was silent for so long she began to wonder if he had detected it and was digesting it. She looked at the heavy cast of his face, apprehensive about the thoughts which lay behind it.

'So Anthony knew you when times were bad,' he finally remarked. 'Is that why you were reluctant to renew your acquaintance with him tonight? He brought back memories you'd rather forget?'

'Yes,' she answered briefly, relieved that his conclusions had fallen short of the whole truth.

Tom glanced at her with a frown of concern. 'Then perhaps this weekend is not such a good idea after all.'

Cathy did not want to back out of the weekend now, she had to go. She put a reassuring smile on her face. 'I've grown up. Things aren't the same as they were then.' She hesitated a moment, then added truthfully, 'It's something I need to face up to, and I'm with you.'

Her last words won a smile which smoothed away his frown. He even began to chuckle, then shook his head in bemusement. 'Tell me how a pharmacy shop-assistant managed to become an expert on antique furniture.'

Her smile held all the satisfaction of achievement. 'A lot of hard work and determination. A chance remark started the idea and I studied up on it, asked a lot of questions and learnt all I could. There's a lot of good antique furniture in the Armidale area. When I was ready I went to auctions and invested all my savings in buying up the best there was. I figured it would sell in Sydney for a good price. Which brought me to you. I was lucky. By all the laws of the business world I should have ended up bankrupt.'

Tom slanted her a look of admiration. 'That took tremendous courage.'

Her grin twisted into a wry grimace. 'Desperation, Tom. When you've had people walking over you, treating you as nothing, you get desperate to make something of yourself. It's either that, or life isn't worth living.'

The matter-of-fact statement drew an oddly determined look from him. 'Nobody will ever do that to you again, Cathy.'

His hand closed more tightly around hers. It gave Cathy a safe, protected feeling. But then Tom had protected her, right from the beginning, suspending interest payments on the capital he had lent until she had established a steady business footing. Protecting his investment he called it, but she doubted that any other investor would have been so patient about seeing some return for his money. She owed him so much more than money could ever repay.

Tom turned the car into the Randwick back street which led to the car-park for her apartment building. Cathy was glad he had brought up the past. If any references were made to it while they were at Mirrima he now had enough information to fit them into place. It would have been wrong to leave him without some understanding of the situation he was walking into with her, although Cathy was reasonably sure that Carlton and Stephanie Pryor-Jones would be all charm in front of Thomas Henry Crawford the Third.

Tom parked the Mercedes in the visitors' bay, helped her out of it with the gentlemanly courtesy which was so natural to him, and escorted her up to her apartment door. Cathy slotted her key into the lock and turned to Tom with a smile which invited his usual embrace.

'Thank you so much for . . .'

'I'd like to come in for a while, Cathy,' he interrupted softly, his eyes pleading her acquiescence.

She hesitated, not liking to refuse him, but feeling too disturbed by her encounter with Anthony to give Tom an uninhibited response to anything more than a goodnight kiss. 'It is late,' she offered in excuse.

'I know. I won't stay long. But there's something important I want to say to you,' he said seriously, and the uncharacteristic tension in his bearing lent weight to the request.

'All right,' she agreed, aware of tension creeping down her own spine.

As she ushered Tom into her living-room she hoped the matter was nothing too serious. She had more than enough on her mind at the moment. 'Would you like a cup of coffee?' she asked, more in nervous agitation than courtesy.

'No, thanks. I just want to talk to you,' he said, taking her arm and drawing her over to an armchair.

She sat down. He pulled the matching armchair

close to hers but he did not sit in it. He propped himself on the armrest and took her nearest hand in his, fondling it nervously. Cathy stared up at him expectantly, her apprehension growing with his obvious unease.

He suddenly gave a little laugh, cutting the cord of tension which had momentarily stretched between them. His eyes glowed down at her with soft indulgence. 'It's nothing very terrible. It's quite simple really. I want you to be my wife.'

He sucked in a sharp breath and continued with barely a pause, his voice husky with emotion. 'I love you, Cathy. It seems to me I've always loved you. I think I fell in love with you the first day we met. But you're such a fiercely independent person and I knew you weren't looking for love for yourself. But the years have changed you, and over the last six months, I think I've become more than a business friend to you. I hope so.'

She could not speak. Shock was still rolling through her, wave after wave of it, cramping her stomach, squeezing her heart in a chest aching with tightness. Her mind seized up completely, locked on the appalling revelation that Tom had loved her all these years. And of all the nights he could have chosen to speak his heart, he had chosen tonight when Anthony had walked out of the past and into the present.

Tom cleared his throat. 'Cathy, will you marry . . .'

'Don't!' The word was a harsh croak. Tears welled into her eyes, forced out by the terrible weight of her dilemma. She pushed herself to her feet and paced blindly away, unable to face the urgent appeal in

Tom's eyes. 'Don't ask me now, Tom. Please! I . . .' She shook her head in helpless distress. 'I can't answer you. Not tonight.'

The tears rolled down her cheeks. If only Anthony had stayed buried in the past she might have said yes, been happy to say yes. Tom was so good to her, so kind, and so very dear, but she could not dismiss Anthony now, could not go forward into a future with Tom with the question of Anthony never completely settled in her mind. It wouldn't be fair on Tom or on herself, maybe not even on Anthony. She just didn't know.

Gentle hands turned her around. She could not look up at him, could not speak. Tears were still squeezing past her long lashes. Her throat was a choking lump of emotion and her lips were quivering so much she bit them in a futile attempt to gain control.

'Don't cry, Cathy,' Tom murmured, and gathered her into a tender embrace. 'Don't cry,' he repeated with a heavy sigh. He pressed her head on to his shoulder and stroked her hair with an unnaturally clumsy hand. 'It's not the end of the world if you say no.'

But she could hear the wretched disappointment in his voice, feel the inner pain through his distracted caress, and her whole body was one searing ache for him. And despite his own distress he cared about hers. It was too much to bear. She had to say something, explain somehow. She dragged her mind for words and spoke in tortured bursts.

'I owe you so much, so much. It seems so terribly unfair, when you've waited so long. But I can't give you an answer tonight. I can't. You do mean a great deal to me, but . . .'

'Hush now. It's all right,' he murmured, his cheek rubbing against her hair in soft comfort. 'Don't be upset. I don't want you to be upset.'

'Oh, Tom, Tom, why are you so good to me?' she cried despairingly.

He tilted her head up and gently kissed her tear-washed eyes shut. 'Because I love you,' he answered. Then gently, 'And I don't want the woman I love crying over me.' He brushed soothing fingers over her trembling lips. 'Please don't be upset.'

She drew in a shuddering breath and attempted a smile which didn't come off. 'I'm sorry. I wasn't expecting it. And . . . and you never said . . .'

His fingers touched her lips again in a silencing gesture. His smile held a twist of self-mockery. 'No, I never said. Maybe I should have. But it's said now. If you don't want me, that's all right. Anything is better than this.'

She realised how deeply she was distressing him and made a concentrated effort to pull herself together. 'Tom, I need to have this weekend before I can make a decision,' she said in a blurted rush. 'It's not that I don't want you. It's . . .' The urge to tell the whole truth was very strong, but if the memories Anthony had stirred proved to be only memories, then she would be putting Tom through unnecessary torment if she revealed them.

She broke away from him and paced around, driven by the torment in her own soul. 'It's something I've got to find out, for my own peace of mind. It wouldn't be fair to make a decision now, not on you or on me.'

She was only hurting him further. She could see it in his eyes, hurt by her inability to give a definite answer and hurt by her evasiveness. It sickened her to the depths of her soul that she had done this to him, but it was too late to retract now, even if she wanted to, and nothing she could do or say would make him feel better.

He heaved a sigh and walked slowly over to her. He took her fluttering hands in his and the restless stroking of his fingers revealed the turbulence of emotion which his calm expression denied. His eyes were shadowed with resignation as he spoke, slowly and with telling emphasis.

'Cathy, a marriage is between two people, a man and a woman. If they love each other enough, then no other considerations really matter, not money or background or social standing or anything else. We've known each other for four years. I've enjoyed every moment that I've spent with you. And whatever happened in your past is totally irrelevant to me. You are the finest person I've ever known.'

He paused to draw breath and his gaze dropped to their hands. His fingers stopped their tortured caress. He shook his head and raised bleak eyes. 'I've tried to tell you this in every way I can. I hoped that tonight would settle whatever reservations you still had in your mind. But now I don't think a weekend of socialising is going to make any difference to the ultimate answer. You don't need to think about love, it either is or it isn't. Thinking about it will only cause us both unhappiness, as it has done tonight. I wouldn't want you as my wife if you didn't love me, so forget my proposal. Thank you for listening to me but forget it ever happened, forget about how I feel. Be happy.'

He summoned up a crooked little smile. 'Tomorrow I'll call for you at one-thirty. We'll drive to the airport and fly up to Mirrima for the weekend. We'll be friends, just as we've always been. We'll enjoy ourselves. And if you need me for anything, I'll always be there.'

She had lost him. He was going to stand by her this weekend and then remove himself from her. She knew it, she knew it as surely as she knew night followed day. She would be alone again, without Tom to lean on, talk to, to share with. Oh what had she done?

He leaned forward and kissed her, but she was all frozen up inside, and his mouth left her unresponsive lips before she could do anything about it.

'Goodbye, Cathy,' he whispered huskily, and turned away from her.

He was at the door before she could whip herself into action. 'Goodnight!' she croaked in rising panic, then practically babbled as she rushed after him, 'It's goodnight, Tom! Not goodbye. Not goodbye. I'll see you tomorrow. One-thirty, you said.'

He turned to her with a travesty of a smile. 'Yes, of course. Goodnight, Cathy.'

He strode off, not stopping at the elevators but making straight for the stairs. He did not glance back. Cathy watched him disappear from view and listened to his footsteps echoing up the stairwell, hurrying, hurrying away from her. And her heart sank lower and lower with each fading sound.

She stepped back inside her apartment and shut the door. For a few minutes she remained leaning against it, dazed by the whole progression of shocks which had hit her tonight. Anthony: was he her real love or a shimmering mirage of the past? He had walked away from her and Tom had entered her life. Now Anthony had returned and Tom had walked away. She shook her head in utter hopelessness, too sick at heart even to try to work out her feelings. The past and the present were all mixed up, a mess. Somehow she was going to have to straighten it all out over this weekend.

Mirrima: such a beautiful place, and as deadly as a Venus fly-trap. Was it a trap for her this time? Would it bring her happiness or a more terrible despair than she had ever known? Cathy undressed and climbed into bed. There was no point in thinking, tomorrow would come soon enough. Tomorrow ... Tom ... Anthony ... Mirrima ...

CHAPTER FIVE

'DONE any flying, Tom?' asked Anthony as they stowed the luggage in the rear compartment of the six-seat Cessna.

'A lot of flying, but not at the controls,' was Tom's matter-of-fact reply.

'Then you haven't flown at all. Come and sit in the co-pilot's seat and I'll give you the experience of your life.'

Tom straightened up, glanced at Cathy as if momentarily reluctant to accept the invitation, then pasted an affable smile on his mouth. 'Fine! I'd like that. But don't give me anything to do until it's perfectly safe.'

Anthony clapped him on the shoulder in friendly approval. 'Safe as a bank. A dream to handle, this plane. Best thing I ever bought.'

'Hey, let me fly it and teach Tom, Anthony,' Vanessa said brightly, turning to take the pilot's seat.

'It's not that safe,' Anthony declared, hauling her back.

Vanessa pouted. 'I thought you'd want to sit with Cathy.'

Tom frowned, Cathy tensed. Anthony's fingers tightened on his sister's shoulder. 'See that Cathy fastens her seat-belt properly, Van. Maybe you can do something right,' he said teasingly.

'Chauvinist pig,' muttered Vanessa but she did not

argue.

Anthony chatted away to Tom as he saw him properly settled in the co-pilot's seat. Vanessa placed Cathy behind Tom and made a pointed action of fastening the belt before taking the companion seat on the other side of the aisle. Anthony flashed Cathy a smile over Tom's shoulder.

'Don't worry, I'll put us into clear sky before handing control to Tom.' The green eyes glittered with excitement but Cathy could not respond to it, sensing a subtle put-down in the reference to Tom.

'I'm not worried at all,' she stated quietly.

'Good!' The smile became a satisfied grin before he turned away to settle himself.

Cathy was finally left to herself and she stared miserably at the back of Tom's head. She did not know how she was going to bear the inevitable tensions of this weekend. Already her nerves were stretched to snapping point.

Tom had done his best to eliminate any strain between them. His fac+acade of cheerful friendliness throughout their trip to Bankstown Airport had been absolutely faultless. Not by word or look had there been the slightest allusion to the night before. Forget it, he had said, and to all appearances he had shut that painful scene out of his mind.

But Cathy could not forget it. For Tom's sake she had responded to his light-hearted conversation in a similar vein, but she had hated every minute of it. Once they had arrived at the airport, Vanessa had claimed Tom's attention, showering him with a vivacious flow of welcome. Cathy had been momentarily relieved by the distraction, only to be stabbed by guilt when Anthony took the opportunity to press his welcome on her.

His compliments on her appearance were strangely bitter-sweet. The pleasure in his eyes had made her heart give a treacherous little skip, but despite the effort and money she had expended on an outfit which was the ultimate in casual sophistication, she wished he had not even noticed her clothes. She did not want Anthony to care about superficial trappings. If he truly loved her, what she wore was totally irrelevant, as irrelevant as it should have been five years ago, as irrelevant as it was to Tom.

The finest person he had ever known. Tom's words echoed through Cathy's mind, making her squirm with shame. She was not fine. Her acceptance of this invitation to Mirrima was totally selfish. She should have backed out of it. If Anthony really did still want her, he could have made some other arrangement to see her again, an arrangement which would not have involved Tom. Only if she stayed cool towards Anthony could she avoid hurting Tom even more deeply.

Her gaze wandered to Anthony's handsome profile and drifted over the thick, sun-bleached hair. How could she stay cool when the mere sight of him completely unsettled her? She watched him start the plane's engines and manipulate the controls with the same confident ease with which he had always manipulated everything, even Tom, who was six years older than he was and certainly no fool.

The noise of the engines was loud enough to inhibit normal conversation. Anthony shouted across to Tom who nodded more times than he yelled back. Vanessa didn't bother with Cathy, for which Cathy was grateful. The time would come soon enough when she would have to cope with polite nothings without having to force them out now.

Vanessa was not the least bit interested in her. Tom, of course, was an entirely different matter. He was worthy of all the attention in the world, and having so recently suffered rejection, it was quite possible that he would find Vanessa's attention very acceptable. Cathy didn't particularly care for that thought. While she berated herself for her dog-in-the-mangerish attitude, she could not dispel her need for Tom's continuing support. She could not even contemplate what her life would be like without it. And yet there was Anthony . . .

Once the plane was in steady flight Vanessa moved to stand between the two men, her hands resting on their seats, effectively forming a closed semi-circle, excluding Cathy. She chattered away to both men but her eyes and smiles were directed mostly to Tom who responded with his usual good humour. Since Anthony had passed the control of the plane to him and was giving the occasional instruction, neither man was in a position to give Cathy his attention. She stared out of the window. The flight droned on. A flight to what? Cathy wondered in silent torment.

'Cathy.'

Anthony's voice drew her attention. He had nudged Vanessa back and his smile was warmly inviting.

'Come and have a flying lesson. Tom will swap seats with you, won't you, Tom?'

'Certainly.' He began unbuckling his belt.

Cathy's heart began a wary flutter as she fumbled with hers. But she wanted Anthony's attention, didn't she? She wanted to know.

'Do you think that's wise, Anthony?' Vanessa drawled in saccharin-sweet concern. 'The last time you and Cathy flew to Mirrima she was pea-green when you arrived!'

Tom was already out of his seat and he instantly shot a sharp, probing look at Cathy. She should have told him. Her stupid, damned reserve about speaking of the past should have been forced aside. He had said it did not matter to him. Now it was too late and God only knew what Vanessa would trot out next.

'That was a smaller plane and we had a very bumpy flight,' Anthony tossed off carelessly.

Cathy pulled herself together and stood up. 'I was also very nervous, having had no experience of flying at all. But I'm not nervous any more, Vanessa.'

Stop feeling guilty, she told herself sternly. She could feel Tom's eyes boring into her as they changed positions but she evaded their silent accusation. She owed Tom a great deal but she did not owe him her life. If she kept shouldering the burden of his feelings, it would obscure her own, and the whole purpose of this visit was to determine what she felt and wanted.

Having dropped her sly little bombshell, Vanessa was happily engaging Tom's attention. With stubborn defiance Cathy shrugged all thought of him away as she strapped herself into the seat he had just vacated. Then with wary blue eyes she glanced at Anthony.

'It won't be like last time,' he promised, and there were layers of meaning injected into the words, reinforced by eyes which held a feverish glitter of need. 'There's only one thing better than flying, Cathy. Only one thing that gives you the same sense of no longer being a separate entity. When you get the feel for it, it becomes part of you and the feeling is unforgettable.'

Unforgettable. There was no doubt what Anthony was talking about . . . their flesh becoming one, to the exclusion of everything else.

'Now take the control-stick in your hand. Feel its power. It's an extension of you, to do with as you will. It responds to your touch. The control is now yours, Cathy. Whenever you want it, take it.'

He was deliberately evoking memories of their lovemaking. His hand reached across and covered hers on the joystick and the caress of his fingers left her in no doubt of what was on his mind. It was on hers too. So strongly that it was all she could do to stop her body from trembling.

'Now just touch the left pedal lightly and then take your foot off it. See what happens.'

She obeyed his instructions unquestioningly. Her heart gave a panicky leap when the plane veered off course. The release of foot pressure brought the flight back on line, but her heart kept thumping an erratic beat as Anthony continued his verbal seduction.

'Pressure turns one off course. Too much pressure and you fly off at a tangent. But left to itself, it will come back. It will come back, Cathy,' he repeated with passionate emphasis.

She glanced into eyes which stripped the years

away and she felt she was with him again, together in the same sense as they had been together before his parents had applied their pressure.

'Share this with me, Cathy,' he urged, and proceeded to take her through a far more comprehensive range of flying routines than he had given Tom.

It was exhilarating, feeling the plane respond to her touch. She was flying, soaring free, and the whole sky was her playground ... with Anthony. His pleasure in her was in every touch, every word, every smile, and excitement bubbled through Cathy's veins and sparkled out of eyes more blue than the sky they were sharing. Tom and Vanessa were forgotten.

'You have a natural touch for it, Cathy, just as you're a natural at everything. I hope you'll want to do this with me again but I'd better take over now. We'll be on the Mirrima boundary any second.'

Mirrima! Cathy came back to relity with a thump. One couldn't live in the clouds. Mirrima was Anthony's reality, his heritage, marked out with very definitive boundaries which Cathy had been unequipped to cross in the past. Whether it would be a different story now was a question which immediately dampened her spirits. With a growing sense of apprehension she watched the rolling plains give way to grazing paddocks on which were dotted rambling flocks of sheep, then field after field of vivid green wheat.

'We're over Mirrima now, Tom,' Vanessa called out excitedly. 'There's the homestead on the horizon. Buzz it before landing, Anthony—I want Tom to see the layout from the air.'

Even though Cathy had seen it all before, the sheer scale of the Mirrima homestead in its magnificent setting was a sight which inspired awe, and fear. It represented unbelievable wealth. Too much wealth. And most of all, jealously guarded wealth.

Looking down at it from this height, one could fully appreciate the ambitious aim of the original architect. The main house lay across the centre of a circle. The two-storeyed stone edifice with its ornate gables and columned verandahs commanded the eye. On its south side was a semi-circular carriageway which serviced the front entrance steps, a carriageway over a hundred years old, and the fountain in its centre still played over statues which had been shipped from Greece in the last century. To the north side of the house was a matching semi-circle formed from paths and gardens and an in-ground pool.

From this central circle, avenues of trees radiated outwards, and in their angles were set the other buildings of the homestead: the summerhouse, the store, office, servants' cottage, stables, barns, machinery-shop, coach-house, garden shed and glass-shouses. At a greater distance away were the woolshed, the workmen's quarters, equipment sheds, the landing-strip and the hangar; and even these outer satellite buildings had been placed to fit into the sun-pattern.

'Well? What do you think of it?' Vanessa demanded of Tom as Anthony wheeled the Cessna towards the landing-strip.

'Incredible to see something like that out here,' he replied slowly, then with a sharp edge of irony, 'I can imagine one might be tempted to marry the land where such a property as this is involved.'

The hairs on the back of Cathy's neck prickled. Had Tom caught the sense of intimacy between her and Anthony or was he merely joking with Vanessa?

'It's not so much the land, Tom, but the whole way of life,' Vanessa boasted proudly. 'There's no place like Mirrima. You couldn't buy it even if you wanted to. It's been in our family for generations.'

'And generations to come,' added Anthony, throwing Cathy an intensely purposeful look before bringing the plane down in a perfect landing.

Cathy's tension returned in full measure as she and Vanessa waited for the men to unload the luggage. A station-wagon was parked in the hangar ready for the short trip to the house. Vanessa opened up the rear compartment ready for the suitcases, ignoring Cathy altogether.

Cathy silently worried over what kind of greeting she would receive from Anthony's parents. They would have been told there were two more guests for the weekend, but had they been informed of her identity? She wished she had thought to question Anthony about it while they were still flying. Apprehension tightened her face as the two men appeared in the doorway of the plane.

Tom emerged first. His gaze swept past Cathy as if she didn't exist; the polite mask of his face was turned to Vanessa. Cathy stared at him, a horrible chill running down her spine as he strode to the station-wagon and deposited his load. Was Tom cutting her dead now, even before the weekend had started?

Cathy's sense of security was severely shaken. It seemed that not even four years of steady building could withstand the force of Mirrima. Like some grotesque and beautiful monument, it dwarfed everything else into insignificance and cast a shadow which warped relationships. She watched Tom return to the plane to take the cases Anthony handed to him. She willed him to look at her but he didn't even glance her way.

Anthony jumped down beside him and swung the door shut. The two men formed a striking contrast; Anthony a head taller than Tom, golden hair shining above an animated face, his athletic physique shown to advantage in cream jeans and a white and cream loose-weave shirt; Tom's solid frame made Anthony appear almost slight in comparison. Dark and stolid, his heavy face expressionless, he looked oddly forbidding. His tailored fawn slacks and brown shirt were too neutral to make any statement of personality. Yet Cathy's heart was torn by so many complex feelings for both men that outward appearances meant nothing.

Vanessa opened the back passenger-door of the station-wagon and the moment Tom's hands were free she dragged him towards it. 'Come and sit next to me, I'll point out everything of interest.'

He seemed to go willingly. Anthony's hand on her elbow snapped Cathy's attention back to him. The green eyes invited her to share his excitement, but tension had Cathy in a strangling grip.

'Do your parents know it's me, Anthony? Did they . . .'

'You need not fear anything from them, Cathy,' he

said with absolute assurance. 'I run Mirrima now. They will be pleased to see you,' his voice took on a hard, ruthless edge, 'if for no other reason than it pleases me.'

It shook her, that hard, ruthless edge. Cathy nursed that disturbing thought as Anthony saw her settled into the front passenger-seat and took his place behind the wheel. The Anthony she had known had not seemed hard in any way. But neither had she been the hard-headed businesswoman she was now. Running a property as huge and diverse in its interests as Mirrima would have necessitated ruthless decision-making, just as the risks she had taken had required steely purpose. The five years had changed both of them.

They were not boy and girl engulfed in young love any more. They were man and woman. The strong, mutual attraction which still existed had to be held at bay until she was sure that she wanted Anthony, the man. Tom's apparent disaffection could not be allowed to confuse her judgement. She was not going to be driven into a premature decision, no matter what consequences would ensue from her actions.

Anthony drove up to the house at a sedate pace, giving Vanessa ample time to draw Tom's attention to the many historic features along the way—the old wych elms and oaks, the cobblestoned approach road, the twisted hedges of wistaria; all received a mention before Vanessa started detailing the house.

'Eleven bedrooms. There used to be seven sitting-rooms, but when Mum had all the plumbing modernised, some of those were taken for bathrooms. The main lounge used to be called the ballroom and it really is great for a formal party. The conservatory is Mum's favourite place and Dad takes most pride in the three cellars.'

Stephanie Pryor-Jones was making a graceful descent of the wide flagstone steps as the station-wagon slowed to a halt. She was still blonde, slim and regal in her tall, perfectly groomed beauty. A green silk dress made the most of her figure, and Cathy knew that the strands of pearls around Stephanie's neck were only casual jewellery to Anthony's mother. The woman still had the power to stir a sense of inferiority in Cathy's heart.

Pride fought it. There was nothing in her own grooming which could be criticised now. The blue skirt and blouse were as well tailored as Vanessa's slack-suit, and the blue and white sandals were a top-class fashion item, as was the matching leather handbag. As for the rest of her appearance, if Vera Pallister had approved it, then Stephanie Pryor-Jones could not find fault.

The polite smile of welcome did not reach the cold, assessing eyes which watched Cathy alight on Anthony's arm. Green eyes, like Anthony's, except that they had never warmed for Cathy. Nor did they now. Cathy met them with a cool reserve of her own, determined not to be intimidated.

'Why, Cathy, how you've changed! I doubt that I would have recognised you if Anthony hadn't told me you were coming.'

The words were coated with sugary charm, but Cathy wasn't fooled. She was no more welcome here than she had been five years ago. She bared her teeth with equal charm. 'You haven't changed at all, Mrs

Pryor-Jones. And once again, it's kind of you to welcome me.'

The genuine, twenty-four-carat gold welcome was switched on for Tom whom Vanessa presented like a prize trophy.

'Tom!' His hands were taken and warmly pressed. 'I'm delighted to meet you and have you visiting Mirrima. I met your people in Melbourne last year when we flew down for Cup Week. We had a lovely evening with them. I do hope you'll enjoy our weekend.'

'How could I not enjoy myself with so much beauty around me?' Tom replied smoothly.

Stephanie gave a pretty trill of laughter and linked her arm with Tom's. 'I can see the Crawford charm is not restricted to the older generation! Come on in and we'll have afternoon tea before you settle into your rooms.'

As they moved through the great hall which bisected the house, Cathy's experienced eye automatically priced the cedar chiffonier, the hall tables and the chests. The grand staircase was virtually priceless and the doors leading off the hall with their beautiful pannelling and stained glass fanlights were rare items. She had felt overwhelmed by the house and its contents on her last visit. Now she could appreciate the full scale of Anthony's inheritance, and it was even more intimidating.

Stephanie led them out to the screened verandah which overlooked the garden around the in-ground pool. They were no sooner settled in comfortable cane armchairs than the housekeeper, Doris Elton, wheeled in a traymobile and proceeded to set out afternoon tea. Her homely, weathered face looked the same, as did the grey frizz of tightly permed hair. Tom was introduced to her and she nodded before turning to Cathy with a smile which seemed warm with satisfaction.

'Pleased to see you again, Miss Cathy. And looking so lovely.'

'Thank you, Mrs Elton,' Cathy replied sincerely, remembering the sympathetic kindness of the old woman as the one soothing pleasantness in a sea of hurt.

'Doris, see that Jacko takes the luggage upstairs, will you?' the mistress of the house commanded sweetly.

Jacko. Cathy remembered him too ... the half-Aboriginal boy who did the odd jobs around the house, a perpetual grin on his dark face. He would be a man now, maybe not so cheerful any more. Cathy had inwardly cringed at the half-exasperated, superior manner Stephanie Pryor-Jones invariably used when giving him orders.

Once the housekeeper had withdrawn, Stephanie showed her formidable skill as a hostess. With a façade of sparkling interest, she set about subtly extracting what information she could about Tom's relationship with Cathy. Tom gave little away, brushing off her questions with general answers and directing the conversation back to life at Mirrima. Cathy followed his lead and took sour satisfaction in frustrating Stephanie's purpose. Five years ago she had naïvely handed over all the ammunition which had helped to blast her hopes of marrying Anthony. The lesson had been learnt: reveal nothing.

'Have you been married, Cathy?'

The unexpected question jolted Cathy out of her complacency.

'No, she hasn't been married, Mother,' Anthony slid in for her, adding with sardonic emphasis, 'no more than I have.'

His mother shot him a hard look before fluttering her hands. 'Oh, the way you play the field, Anthony, I doubt you'll ever settle down. But Cathy . . . well, you're so different, my dear. And you must have needed a lot of capital to go into the antique trade.'

Angry fire burnt into Cathy's cheeks but she managed to project a lightly mocking voice. 'There are other ways of getting capital besides marrying it, Mrs Pryor-Jones. As it happened, Tom's investment company lent the finance necessary for me to break into the Sydney market. The fact is that investment companies are prepared to take a chance on people now and then. Isn't that so, Tom?'

Her eyes stabbed at him defiantly and she was surprised to actually meet his gaze. It was the first time since they had arrived at Mirrima that he had looked directly at her. The brown eyes which had always been soft for her were narrowed into hard, speculative slits.

'Yes, that's so,' he stated flatly. 'Cathy's enterprise proved to be very successful.'

Stephanie pounced on the opening. 'Oh, then you've known each other for a long time?'

'That rather depends on what you mean by knowing each other,' Tom answered with an ironic twist. 'But we have been business associates for four years, which is quite a long time.'

'Ages!' Vanessa drawled dismissively. 'If you've finished your tea, Tom, I'll show you your room and help you unpack. Which guest-room, Mum?'

'The corner suite, dear. And Cathy, you're in the same room you had before.'

'No!' Anthony clipped in decisively. 'I told you Cathy was to have the Victorian suite.'

'But, dear, the Lachlans are arriving tonight and they always have . . .'

'Not this time. This time will be different. And I hope there won't be any misunderstandings on that score, Mother.' Anthony stood up, his handsome face hard with a commanding arrogance. 'I'll show Cathy to her suite and you can make whatever other arrangements you like for the Lachlans.'

Cathy pushed herself to her feet, a self-conscious blush on her cheeks as she sought to reduce the electric tension in the room. 'Please, I don't want to put anyone out, Anthony. I'm quite . . .'

He overrode her attempt at peace-making. 'You're not putting anyone out, Cathy. And no one's putting you out. I hope that is clear now, Mother.'

Stephanie gritted her teeth and gave a resigned shrug. 'As you wish, Anthony.'

Vanessa jumped up and urged Tom to his feet, chattering non-stop to smooth over the awkwardness caused by Anthony's all-too-pointed stance over Cathy's position. Anthony himself was not the least bit concerned about any feathers he might have ruffled. Cathy bit her lip and said nothing, knowing that any further argument would only aggravate the matter. Anthony took her arm and virtually swept her back into the hall, up the staircase, and into a huge guest-room, furnished with an awesome array of magnificent furniture and accessories, and featuring as its centrepiece an imposing four-poster double bed.

'Antique,' he grinned at her. 'I thought you'd like sleeping in it.' He gathered her into his embrace and suddenly his eyes were a blaze of triumph and desire. 'With me, Cathy. Always with me.'

Panic spilled out a protest. 'Anthony, you're assuming too much. I don't . . .'

His lips brushed hers. 'Love me, Cathy. Love me like you used to.'

She tried to speak, but the words choked in her throat as Anthony took avid possession of her mouth. Cathy's resolve to keep him at arm's length for a while was instantly shattered. The emotional turmoil he had triggered last night demanded release, with instinct swamping reason in a clawing need to know exactly how deep was her response to Anthony, if she was still prepared to give the total surrender he had always drawn from her. Her passion was born of desperation but Anthony did not question it. His own passion flared into a feverish onslaught of kisses which had Cathy swimming in a turbulent world of sensation.

The knock on the door shocked her back to reality. She pushed at Anthony in horrified agitation. He held her to him with relentless strength. 'Who is it?' he demanded curtly.

'Jacko, Boss. With Miss Cathy's suitcases.'

Anthony relaxed his embrace a little but still did not release her. 'Right, Jacko, bring them in.'

The door opened. Cathy barely saw Jacko's

grinning face. There was another face behind it, and the look in Tom's eyes shrivelled her soul.

CHAPTER SIX

'HERE y'are, Miss Cathy,' Jacko said brightly, carrying the suitcases into the room.

Tom followed him in and came to a stiff halt just past the doorway. His gaze dropped to Cathy's hands, still resting upon Anthony's shoulders. After a long, fixed stare it slid lower, to fasten on to the arms which held her in a possessive embrace, then down to the clinging pressure of thighs against thighs. His face froze, all colour draining into a pasty grey. Only his eyes shone with life, and they projected the glittering deadliness of a cobra waiting to strike.

'Maybe you want to race me again in the swimming-pool, Miss Cathy,' Jacko prattled on. 'I swim very fast now.'

'Hop it, Jacko,' Anthony commanded tersely.

'Yes, Boss.' He backed towards the door, beaming and bobbing his head. 'Just being friendly, Boss. I remember Miss Cathy from last time. She . . .' Then as if suddenly struck by the cross-waves of tension, he clammed up, rolled his eyes, skipped past Tom and shut the door on the three of them.

Cathy had barely registered Jacko's presence, barely heard his words. Like a tableau in a play, she and Tom and Anthony were frozen in their places, waiting. She knew it was too late to move away from Anthony, to spare Tom's feelings. She was caught,

suspended in guilt, and Tom's eyes were searing her
with accusation. For what seemed an interminable
age no one spoke. Anthony pulled her more firmly
against him and the movement triggered an instant
reaction from Tom.

His eyes flared at Cathy. His nostrils pinched with
a sharply indrawn breath. 'You should have told me.'
His voice was strange, harsh, cutting in its wintry
chill.

She should have. She should have been more
open with him. But she hadn't expected, hadn't fore-
seen . . .

The blazing anger gathered bitter contempt as
Tom's gaze swung up and bored savagely into
Anthony. 'You both set me up beautifully, didn't
you?'

'No,' Cathy gasped, horrified that he had inter-
preted her reticence as a kind of conspiracy. 'Tom,
no!' she declared more vehemently, her eyes pleading for a stay of judgement as she struggled against
Anthony's hold.

Tom ignored her, his whole being wound into
barely controlled aggression as he delivered a
scathing indictment. 'Your show of good will to me
last night, Anthony . . . faultless, yet so contemptibly
false. The concern over Cathy's not having a
holiday, that was a brilliant touch. And Cathy's
apparent reluctance to come . . . that took me right
in. Completely fooled! God Almighty! So completely fooled!' He shook his head in self-disgust before
resuming his bitter attack. 'But then I've never met
anyone so totally unprincipled as you, Anthony.
What pleasure did you get from it?'

His eyes suddenly stabbed at her. 'And I thought I knew you, Cathy, God help me, how could I have been so wrong? You . . .'

'Shut up, Tom!' Anthony cut in with threatening ferocity. 'Say one more word against Cathy and I'll ram it down your throat.'

Tom's hands clenched into fists.

'No, please,' begged Cathy, wrenching herself out of Anthony's embrace and taking a preventive stance between the two men. Her hands instinctively lifted in mute appeal to Tom. 'It wasn't like that. It was . . . it was . . . 'She floundered hopelessly in the face of grim rejection.

'Why the hell did you have to use me? So meanly!' he grated out with intense bitterness.

'Cathy didn't use you. I did,' Anthony stated without an ounce of shame.

He moved to curve a protective arm around Cathy's shoulders. She shuddered, recoiling from the image of being linked with Anthony, yet too shaken to push herself away from his support. He continued speaking with a calm ruthlessness which shook her even more.

'I would have used anyone or anything to get Cathy back here with me. And I don't give a damn what you think, Tom. Where Cathy is concerned, you're a Johnny-come-lately. I loved her five years ago and I've never stopped loving her. She was mine long before she met you and she's mine now.'

'No.' The word was barely a croak. Cathy gulped in air as she once more dragged herself away from Anthony. 'No, I'm not,' she got out with more force, her eyes darting frantically to Tom before challenging Anthony's certainty with snapping resentment. 'I'm not yours or anyone's. I need time, Anthony. And you're rushing me into . . .'

'Don't take any notice of him!' Anthony cut in harshly, grasping her upper arms and pulling her back to stamp his physical domination on her as he poured out a passionate defence. 'I love you and you love me. And our love is beyond judgement or criticism, beyond your friendship with Tom, beyond my duty to my family. It's you and me, Cathy. Together we can stand against anything because our love transcends everything.'

Tom's bark of derision snapped the powerful thread of Anthony's speech. 'And where has this great love of yours been for the last five years?' he mocked savagely.

'Get out!' Anthony shot at him. 'Go back to Vanessa. She may want you, but we don't. You don't understand a damned thing!'

'Don't I? I know you're a bloody liar,' Tom retorted with scathing contempt. 'No man who loves a woman would have abandoned her as you did. When I met Cathy she was an emotional cripple.'

'And you think I wasn't?' Anthony flashed back fiercely. 'God! You don't know what you're talking about!'

It jolted Tom. The grim certainty in his eyes wavered. He glanced sharply at Cathy and the certainty returned, as hard as stone. 'No. You've played me for a fool once, Anthony. You can't do it again. You don't care about anyone but yourself. You might be able to pull the wool over Cathy's eyes,

but let me warn you, if you take her love and hurt her
again as you did before, I'll crucify you!'

The vehement passion in the threat stunned
Cathy. Never had she heard Tom speak with such
forceful emotion, not even last night. While she had
not doubted his love for her, it had seemed a gentle,
caring love, not the kind of life-and-death passion
which had just exploded from him. It more than
stunned her; it appalled her that she had been so
lacking in perception.

He strode for the door. The ache of loss which
Cathy had been nursing all day suddenly billowed
into intolerable pain. She could not let him go. She
had to explain. She needed his understanding, his
forgiveness, his . . .

Dark, forbidding eyes stabbed back at her as he
opened the door. 'So this was what you were driving
yourself towards, all along. I was waiting for the
impossible, wasn't I?'

His bitterness pierced her heart. 'No, no, no!' she
cried in desperate protest, and tore herself out of
Anthony's grasp. Her chest heaving with tortured
emotion she turned anguished eyes from one man to
the other. 'Please don't go, Tom. Please, I beg you.
Anthony, I want to talk to him alone. You've got to
give me time. I can't cope with this, I can't!'

Again no one moved, no one spoke. The tension
screamed through Cathy. She was sick with it, faint
with it. Anthony stepped forward, shrugging off the
conflict with a complete change of manner. He gave
her shoulder a light, reassuring squeeze and smiled
into her frantic eyes.

'Of course you should talk to Tom, Cathy. He's

your friend.' His hand lifted from her shoulder and tenderly cupped her cheek. 'But don't forget I'm the man you love, always and for ever, just as I love you.' Then still smiling, he walked past Tom, gesturing an affable invitation for him to stay. The door was closed with quiet control.

Cathy breathed again, but there was no relaxation of tension from Tom. The grim set of his face did not relax one iota and his eyes were hard coals of darkness, conceding nothing.

'Is there anything left to say?' he demanded harshly.

His bristling antagonism deterred any conciliatory move. Cathy's hands fluttered in a defeated gesture of appeasement. 'Please, will you listen to me, Tom? I want to explain.'

He might have been granite for all her appeal moved him. Nothing, not the slightest spark of receptivity.

'You don't need to explain anything, Cathy,' he replied, cutting her dead.

'I didn't plan this!' she cried despairingly. 'I didn't plan any of it. I swear that's the truth, Tom.'

He remained rigid. 'You could have prevented it. One word was sufficient.'

The sin of omission, and it had been a grievous sin, there was no denying it, no excusing it. For a moment despair had her paralysed. Then the need to reach Tom drove her forward, instinct overriding reason as she grabbed his hand and held on, despite his stiff resistance to her touch. 'I did try to say no. You know I did,' she babbled urgently. 'But then I thought . . . I thought . . .'

'You thought of Mirrima and all it entails,' Tom finished savagely, throwing off her hold and striding across the room to the window. He swept the heavy silk curtains aside and turned to her, his eyes biting with mockery. 'Look at it! Mirrima is the top of the tree, isn't it? Stupid not to take one more chance at it, now that you can hold your own in any society, which means so damned much to you!'

'That's not how it is, Tom.'

He made a curt, guttural sound of disgust. 'Come on, Cathy! This is where it started. I've worked it all out, so there's no sense in denying it. Anthony brought you here five years ago, and ever since then you've been clawing your way up to the kind of life it represented to you. It's all you've thought of. Nothing else would satisfy you, not even all the Crawford wealth. It just couldn't offer you enough to match this,' he added with bitter self-mockery.

'Don't say that! Don't think it!' Cathy exclaimed in terrible agitation. 'You're so wrong! So wrong!' she repeated, feeling hopelessly inadequate for the task of putting him right.

'Then tell me where I'm wrong,' he challenged, dropping the curtain and eyeing her with hard scepticism.

'It's not you, or position, or wealth, or anything like that,' she rushed out, then shook her head in helpless frustration. 'You don't know what it was like back then. I had nothing but Anthony. He was my life, my whole life. Then he brought me here and they destroyed it all. I hate this place. I *hate* it!'

Tears glittered in her eyes as she plunged on, memories and emotions clawing their way out, stripping her raw. 'I wanted to die. There was no one left to care about, no one to care for me. My parents had thrown me out for going with Anthony. His parents had cut me out of Anthony's life. They all saw me as bad. And I hated the whole rotten world so much I . . .'

She broke off, gritting her teeth until the choking wave of despair was driven back by steely determination. Only then could she speak and the words burst from her with explosive force. 'Don't you see I had to beat it? I had to make the world accept me as someone, someone worth something!'

Even to Cathy's ears, the echo of those words sounded plaintive, empty. If they had touched Tom at all she saw no sign of it. He stood there as unmoved as a judge at an inquisition.

'So what is this? Some kind of revenge for the past?' he demanded coldly.

She stared miserably at him, biting her lips against the truth which would surely build an even more formidable wall between them. She could not bear to watch that happen. She dragged her feet over to the bed and sat down. Her shoulders slumped in defeat as she hung her head and shook it slowly from side to side. Her mind performed a futile search for words to spare Tom further hurt, there were none.

'No, it's not revenge. I wanted to see if I could stand up to Anthony's mother. I wanted to know if I could still be intimidated by Mirrima. It was like a test of the mettle I've forged for myself since I was last here. Something I had to prove for my own self-respect.' Shame, pride, she didn't know what, but some sense dictated that she lift her head and meet

Tom's eyes as she gave him the only critical truth.
'And I had to find out if I still loved Anthony.'

He flinched as though she had struck him. His jaw
tightened and his voice lashed back at her with angry
pain. 'Why didn't you tell me that last night? Why
did you have to drag me along to watch you? Have
you no feelings? No humanity? Don't you think you
could have spared me this? Why did you have to
involve me? It's so . . .' His teeth clamped down on
the words, but his eyes were more than eloquent in
accusing her of wanton torture. He spat out one last
damning word. 'Why?'

Impossible to explain the groping, agonising
indecision which had robbed her of any clear-
sightedness. She had been totally selfish, totally. And
there was no other course but to speak the truth. In a
small, wretched voice she answered him. 'I wanted
. . . I needed you with me.'

His mocking laugh choked in his throat. His eyes
held wild disbelief. 'You wanted me to hear a man
making verbal love to you? You wanted me to see
you in another man's arms? You needed me for that?
Do you want me to hold your hand while you make
love to him as well?'

She was on her feet, her hands over her ears, and
she was shouting, 'Stop it! Stop it!' before her inner
turmoil subsided enough for control to be grasped at.
She lowered her hands and wrung them in an effort
to stop the shaking. She took quick, shallow breaths
to counteract the painful thumping of her heart. And
all the time her eyes begged Tom's patience and
searched for some little softening. There was none.
'You don't understand,' she whispered weakly.

Tom's mouth thinned and he threw up his hands in contemptuous dismissal. 'Everybody's telling me I don't understand. What is it I don't understand, that my ears don't hear, that my eyes don't see?' The dripping sarcasm was accompanied by sharp, cutting gestures. 'Well, I'll tell you what I understand, Cathy. One dance with Anthony last night, one dance that you weren't even keen to have . . . only one dance, and all the feeling which had developed between us is over.'

He shook a fist at her and opened the fingers in a derisive gesture. 'Gone! Four years of sharing, of being together, just evaporated, as if it were nothing. That's what I mean to you. Nothing.' His lips curled in disgust. 'And you didn't have the guts to tell me. Oh, I understand all right—only too well. I'm of so little account to you that you would let me suffer seeing another man make love to you. God!'

'Tom, please, please listen to me.'

Cathy threw herself after him as he turned away from her. He tried to shrug her off, but she clung on until he stopped walking and faced her. Still she was afraid to let him go. Her fingers scrabbled over his chest, gathering his shirt into hand-holds.

'I didn't mean to hurt you, Tom,' she gabbled breathlessly. 'Please believe me. I didn't want it to happen. I didn't want Anthony to . . . to get to me again. It hurt so much last time. I thought with you I could resist the old attraction, that it was just a memory, and I could put it away. But I wasn't sure. And I couldn't give you the answer you wanted until I *was* sure.'

Her eyes darted frequently to his as she spilled out

the whole wretched turmoil Anthony had sparked, hoping against hope that she would break through to Tom's generous heart. 'I couldn't help it. He made me remember how it was. I belonged to him, Tom, so utterly and completely that my heart only beat because he was there. He was everything to me. And I died when he left me. You know a different woman, Tom. One built out of the remains. But he still calls to me. He takes me in his arms and before I know it I'm responding just as I used to. I can't think. It's all wild, pulsing feeling that just sweeps away all common sense. He takes control and I'm helpless. I . . .'

Suddenly his hands closed over her shoulders and he shook her. 'Anthony is a taker! Can't you see that?' he grated in raging frustration. He stopped shaking her and a ripple of horror crossed his face. 'Damn you, Cathy! Damn you! I've wanted you for years, dreaming of you, waiting for you, caring for you. And now you tell me you might be in love with a . . . a man without integrity!'

His fingers were moving convulsively, kneading her soft flesh, and the reserve in his eyes melted into a furnace of naked hunger. Cathy was mesmerised by that hunger. It was so fierce and so alien to anything she had ever seen before in Tom's eyes. It gripped her heart, stopped it, squeezed it.

Tom's breathing grew harsh as he spoke. 'You want a taker? Is that what excites you? Having a man run roughshod over all your inhibitions? Is that what you find irresistible, Cathy?'

She opened her mouth to deny it but Tom was beyond being denied. One hand slid to the pit of her back, thrusting her against him. The other entwined itself in the curls at the back of her head, forcing enough tilt for his mouth to swoop on hers in a hard, punishing kiss. There was no tenderness, no wish to give pleasure or take it. He ground her body against his as he ground his mouth into hers, fiercely, with a raw, barbaric passion which was frightening.

It wasn't Tom. Panic burst through Cathy's veins. She fought the rampaging stranger with every ounce of strength she had left, beating at him, twisting, clawing, until she was free of him. Then they stared wildly at each other, their chests heaving, their faces drawn into shattered masks of their former selves.

'So now we both know, don't we?' rasped Tom. 'You melt for him but not for me. So take him. You deserve him for what you've done to me. Never in my whole life have I lost control of myself like this. Never! If you have any decency left, Cathy, any consideration for me at all, don't flaunt your passion for him in front of me!'

He drew back his shoulders, forced a taut composure into his facial muscles, lifted his chin, then with the proud bearing which comes to men after generations of dignified success, he strode to the door and opened it.

Cathy watched him with bleak, empty eyes. There was no move left to make. There was no way now they could even be friends.

Tom half turned, looking over his shoulder, a long, hard, scathing look. 'I hope you find contentment in your choice, Cathy,' he said stiffly, then shut the door firmly behind him.

CHAPTER SEVEN

HER choice: Tom's words mocked the sickening maelstrom of emotions which were sapping Cathy's ability to make any decision about anything. She had not made a choice. It was Tom who had chosen.

She lifted a trembling hand to her forehead and pushed away the curls. Her skin felt clammy and there was a buzzing dizziness in her head. There was no point in staring at a shut door, she thought wearily. Better to sit down and try to pull herself together.

Her legs felt like jelly as she took the few tottering steps to the bed. She resisted the temptation to lie down and bury her head in a pillow. This was not a time to give in to weakness, however weak she felt. The weak went under at Mirrima. She was not going to let that happen again. If nothing else, she would hold her head high this weekend.

She wished she could have made Tom understand. The pain in her heart sharpened. He wouldn't listen to her any more. But what more could she have said or done, given the circumstances as they had occurred. She heaved a sigh to relieve the constriction in her chest. It was no use stewing over it now. She felt badly enough without further torturing herself with 'if onlys'. She had not meant to deceive Tom. She had not wanted to hurt him in any way. She had done her best to explain. All to no avail, except to hurt him even more deeply.

She closed her eyes and rubbed at the lids, needing to dim the all-too-sharp memory of Tom's face after that horrible, abortive attempt to arouse her. It hadn't been Tom, not the Tom who had grown into her life so gradually she hadn't realised how deeply embedded he was in it, until the brutal surgery of those last few minutes.

Cathy took a deep breath and opened her eyes. She had to face up to the dismal truth that she couldn't depend on Tom for anything now. Decency and consideration dictated that she stay as far away from him as possible, and not flaunt her passion for Anthony. Her mouth curved into a wry grimace. She didn't even know if she had a passion for Anthony.

She wondered if a woman ever really got over her first lover—her only lover, Cathy corrected with a heavy heart—particularly when that lover was intimately connected to the most traumatic period of her life. Maybe Anthony would always have the power to evoke an emotional reaction. That did not necessarily mean that she still loved him.

The knock on the door broke into her maundering reverie, snapping her nerves taut again.

'Cathy!'

Anthony's voice. She relaxed. At least Anthony loved her, or said he did. He had fought for her against Tom's anger and she had been grateful for the timely and gracious exit he had made, despite the dreadful scene which had followed. Her shattered sense of worth needed the soothing balm of Anthony's attention.

'Come in,' she called, pushing herself to her feet

and hoping she did not look as wrung out as she felt.

Anthony came in; tall, springy, vital, exuding an inner excitement which shone out of his eyes. His smile of pleasure dimmed as his gaze took in her white face and the unopened suitcases which were still where Jacko had placed them.

'Torrid old meeting,' he said lightly.

Cathy's smile was a wobbly attempt to match his mood. 'You could say that.'

He pulled a sympathetic grimace and shook his head as he strolled over to take her hands. 'Poor Cathy,' he murmured, his eyes drawing the suffering from hers. 'Such moments can't be anything but hurtful to everyone. I know how it feels. But there comes a time when one has to face facts, and Tom should be grown up enough to do that. I'm sorry for him. But I love you.'

He lifted her hands to his shoulders, then ran feather-light fingertips down her forearms on his way to sliding his arms around her waist. 'Dear Cathy,' he sighed as he drew her closer. 'It's so good to touch you—the fineness of your skin, the silkiness of your hair, the sensual curve of your back, the wonderful way your whole body fits to mine. I never forgot any of it, but to feel you like this again, so close to me. It makes nonsense of dreams.'

It did feel good to be held and gently caressed. Cathy sagged against Anthony's strong body and took comfort from his petting. It did not excite her but it helped to fill the chill, hollow places that Tom had left.

'Better now?' he murmured, seductively nuzzling her ear.

'Yes,' she breathed, then pulled away enough to discourage any more seductive maneouvres. She did not want to fight Anthony off too.

He smiled down at her. 'Then let me help you unpack. You haven't even started, and I want you to look especially beautiful for me tonight.'

An ironic little smile tugged at her mouth. 'Do you think it will make any difference to your parents' opinion of me?'

He laughed and planted a kiss on her nose. 'If you came down in rags I still wouldn't care what they thought. For my pleasure only, my love.'

He released her and swung the suitcases up on the bed, clicking them open before Cathy had even moved. The distinctive drone of an aeroplane distracted him from removing the tissue paper from the dress she had planned to wear tonight.

'Damn! That sounds like the Partridges' plane and they're bringing the Rileys with them.' He shot Cathy a sardonic look. 'The parents' old-time friends. I promised to help transport them to the house. Can you manage here? Shall I send Lucy up with an ironing-board?'

'Lucy?'

'Jacko's young sister. She's on the house-staff now.'

Cathy shook her head. 'I don't need any help, Anthony.'

'Sure?' He drew her into his embrace once again. 'You have only to ask for anything, and I'll get it for you.'

It wasn't bravado, he meant it. And his determination to please her was heartwarming. 'I'm fine, truly.

I brought uncrushable clothes,' she assured him with the first real smile she had managed since Tom had left.

'Good. Dinner's at eight. Drinks in the lounge from seven onwards. Come down when you're ready. There'll be fourteen at table, but it won't be very formal. This is always a fairly casual weekend. And it won't be a drawn-out affair because tomorrow night's the real party. Okay?'

She nodded.

His eyes glowed down at her, desire kindling in the green depths. 'Kiss me, Cathy,' he commanded huskily. 'Kiss me with all your heart.'

She kissed him. But not with all her heart. The sensual excitement which Anthony was so skilled at arousing tingled under her skin and the temptation to pursue it tickled her mind, but a self-protective wall of reserve held firm. Not yet, it said.

Anthony seemed satisfied with her response. 'That will have to last me until tonight. Don't be late down, will you? Time without you is meaningless.'

She felt flattered and pleasured by that thought long after Anthony had left her. She went about the task of unpacking mechanically, wondering if she was a fool to hold back from Anthony. Tom was lost to her anyway. What was she holding back for? She was here to satisfy herself, wasn't she? And maybe she would only learn what she wanted to know if she let Anthony make love to her.

The four-poster bed started dominating her thoughts as much as it dominated the room. Did the answer she needed lie there? Anthony had suggested she share it with him. Did he expect to sleep with her tonight? Memories flooded back: Anthony's naked body curved around hers, Anthony poised above her, his face strained with passion, both of them trembling with anticipation, their bodies entwined in the clinging aftermath of satiation, united, a world unto themselves.

But there was more to love than bed, Cathy reminded herself, and determinedly turned her back on it, gathering up fresh underclothes and going to the *en suite* bathroom. Its extravagant size suggested that this might have been one of the sitting-rooms taken over when Stephanie had all the plumbing modernised. Certainly there was nothing antiquated about the facilities. Cathy showered, then settled herself at the marble-topped vanity table.

A blow-dryer quickly restored the few damp tendrils of hair into shining bounciness. Her make-up took longer. The red dress she had bought demanded a more daring use of colour, but she was careful to underplay the effect she wanted. Enough but nothing too obvious, she decided when she was satisfied.

Two more aeroplanes had landed while she had been in the bathroom. Cathy glanced at the domed pendulum clock on the chest of drawers as she returned to the bedroom. It was past seven already, but dressing would only take up a few more minutes. She quickly pulled on an ultra-fine pair of tights, the underslip of her dress, then finally the dress itself.

A scarlet woman, she thought with amused irony, as she surveyed herself in the mirror. A Jezebel, her father would have said. Cathy frowned. The thought had just popped into her head. It had all been so

unfair and she did not want to remember things like
that. Besides, the dress was positively demure in
style and not all scarlet. The subtle intermingling of
tones ran to a deep magenta. It was an Italian dress
with graceful, flowing lines, and Cathy's slimness
and height carried it off to perfection.

She fastened her one good piece of jewellery
around her neck, a garnet pendant in an antique gold
setting. She had bought it at an auction of a deceased
estate and knew she had been lucky enough to get a
tremendous bargain. Its unusual and beautiful
craftsmanship stamped it as quality and it was the
ideal complement to her dress. Finally she slipped on
the elegant, high-heeled sandals of magenta suede
and set off to face the exacting company downstairs.

She met no one on her way. Even before she
reached the foot of the stairs she could hear the cross-
threads of conversation in the lounge-room whose
double doors were wide open. An attack of nerves
had her step faltering for a moment. No doubt she
would be facing the élite of the countryside. What
were their names? Partridge, Riley, Lachlan, and
another couple if there were to be fourteen at table.
She took courage from the fact she had passed Vera
Pallister's eye and walked a steady, proud line into
the lounge-room.

It had the dimensions of a ballroom and the
polished parquet flooring gleamed richly around the
beautiful Persian rugs. The party had arranged itself
towards the far end where a magnificent cedar fire-
surround dominated the centre of the wall. Cathy
had no time to admire the paintings or the furniture.
She was making a quick assessment of the other

women's evening attire, and her eyes found relief in the fact that she was indeed suitably dressed.

'Ah, Cathy,' Anthony breathed in satisfaction from the other end of the room, directing everyone's attention towards her.

Interested eyes everywhere, except Tom's. He was there, propped on the armrest of Vanessa's chair, but his back remained turned to Cathy. She bleakly noted the rigid stillness of his back. She understood all too well why he wouldn't want to see her, particularly not her and Anthony together. And in a way, his turned back was a release for her because it allowed her to concentrate on her feelings for Anthony without being distracted by concern for Tom.

Anthony walked slowly towards her, as if mesmerised, his face alight with pleasure. His voice was pitched low, but every syllable was slowly and clearly articulated, and even though the words were directed solely at her, they were audible to any listener. 'How very beautiful you look tonight.' His hands reached for hers, clasping them gently in his own as he stood back and shook his head in mute admiration.

His voice softened even further, yet the rich, mellow tone still carried. 'Never have I seen you look so perfect, radiant, bewitching. And all for me. Waiting for you becomes exquisite pleasure when the result is so enchanting.'

He drew her close and linked her arm through his, whispering, 'This is how I want to walk through life. Together with you.' And his eyes held more than approval, more than satisfaction, more than admiration. They surely glowed with love.

Cathy was stunned. She had not expected such a fervent and public declaration of interest from Anthony. The confidence she had manufactured for herself was a weak, defensive thing compared to the explosion of buoyant feelings Anthony had set off with his greeting. He led her forward with such an air of pride that no one could possibly take her as anything but a guest of the utmost importance to him, here, at Mirrima, where she had been made to cringe for her inferiority.

'I am honoured. And very proud to be able to introduce you to some old friends of the family,' Anthony declared with even more fervour.

It was easy for Cathy to smile with pleasure as the introductions were effected. The smiles she received held not the slightest trace of condescension. They beamed with interest and approval. She even had the gratification of hearing Mary Lachlan whisper to her husband, 'What a stunningly attractive girl!' And Ted Lachlan's reply, 'Smashing.'

Curran was the fourth name she had to remember, Anne and Bill Curran. They all seemed very charming people, and to Cathy's utter astonishment none more charming than Stephanie and Carlton Pryor-Jones when Anthony had completed the formalities.

Carlton took her hands, his eyes warm with welcome and appreciation. He had worn a constant frown for her five years ago, but the distinguished, still handsome face was full of bluff heartiness tonight. 'My dear, I can only echo Anthony's sentiments. You would enhance any company, and it's a very great pleasure to have you here at Mirrima with us.'

'Thank you,' murmured Cathy, wondering if she had achieved this totally unexpected reception with her changed appearance, or if Anthony's stance had pressured his father into public acceptance of her.

But Carlton went one step further. 'Before you go back to Sydney, I'd like to get to know you better, Cathy. But I suppose that's too much to hope for with Anthony around.'

'I might lend her to you for a dance tomorrow night, Dad. I guess I owe you that much,' Anthony conceded with a teasing show of reluctance.

'What a lovely necklace, Cathy!' exclaimed Stephanie, her face expressing the first delight Cathy had ever seen on it. 'It must be antique. Those old settings are lovely, aren't they?' She turned to Mary Lachlan with an eager flow of interest. 'Cathy owns an antique shop in Paddington, The Cedar Heritage. Next time we fly to Sydney, you must come and look through it with me, Mary.'

Cathy gave a little shake of her head to clear it of incredulity. It was difficult to accept what was happening. But it was happening; Anthony's parents were publicly accepting her.

'I'd love to,' Mary Lachlan replied warmly.

Cathy found her voice. 'Mrs Pryor-Jones, what you have here can't be matched anywhere. I doubt that I could supply anything better than what you already own.'

'Well, I'd like to see anyway. And Cathy, I would prefer it if you'd call me Stephanie.'

Cathy's mind boggled. She smiled and nodded

automatically, completely lost for words. This had to be all Anthony's doing. The difference between Stephanie's greeting this afternoon and her attitude to Cathy now was a remarkable volte-face for anyone, and even more remarkable in a Pryor-Jones. There had to have been an awful lot of forceful talking done behind the scenes since she had arrived, and obviously Anthony's opinion had carried the most weight.

Anthony's gentle squeeze on her arm helped bring her back to earth a little. She looked up at him with dazed eyes and sparkling happiness looked back at her. Happiness and love? Her stunned heart began pumping an erratic tune.

'You'll find a lot of things have changed at Mirrima since you were last here. Not so much in the externals, they only change with the seasons. But they have in other ways. I hope you approve of them. I want you to enjoy being here with me, Cathy.'

In his own way, Anthony was quietly and effectively telling her that the hurts of the past would not be repeated. He seated her next to Mary Lachlan, fetched her a drink, offered her a tray of hors d'oeuvres, and generally directed such a concentrated stream of attention on her that Cathy felt completely overwhelmed by it.

Even in the old days Anthony had not been this intense, except where sex was concerned. Maybe she had misjudged him, placing the blame for their separation totally at his door. It could have been partly her fault. Her own lack of self-assurance in the company that was natural to a Pryor-Jones might have contributed heavily towards misunderstanding. She did not lack that now. Under Tom's guidance she had climbed to the top and could hold her own anywhere.

Tom! Her eyes darted towards him. He was sitting on the other side of the room, apparently deep in conversation with Vanessa. Cathy sighed with relief. She had had no time to feel concern over Tom since Anthony had taken her over with his greeting. She had so many other feelings . . . relief, amazement, elation, triumph, excitement . . . there just wasn't room for anything else.

It was not until Anthony's parents led the move to the dining-room and arranged the placings at the table that Cathy was forcibly reminded of Tom's cold shoulder. The two young couples were seated across from each other at the centre of the table, Vanessa facing Cathy, Tom facing Anthony. But although Tom's face was looking at them, the eyes were not, and they very pointedly avoided doing so. Cathy was suddenly very, very aware of what Tom had to be feeling and guilt shadowed her pleasure.

She reached for her serviette but Anthony forestalled her, smilingly taking it, removing the silver ring, unfolding the small square of embroidered white linen and spreading it on her lap. A self-conscious flush filtered into Cathy's cheeks as he performed the intimate little courtesy. She hoped Tom had not noticed it. She did not want to cause him any further pain, and she would do everything in her power to avoid doing so.

She glanced across at him. His gaze appeared to be on Carlton who was moving down Cathy's side of the table, filling glasses with a chilled white wine. The dark eyes suddenly swept past Cathy as if she did not exist. She stared at him, the flush draining out of her cheeks as her own eyes gathered the telling evidence of a jaw set too tightly, muscles under strain. Then slowly, as if compelled by a force he could not control, his head turned back to her until their eyes locked over the table.

There was no anger, no hate, no feeling at all in those dark eyes. They seemed completely dead, void of all expression. His face was completely still, shut down, blanketed of all feeling. A muscle suddenly spasmed near his cheekbone. His chin moved fractionally and Cathy sensed the struggle behind the wooden mask, the need to turn away, the innate pride of the man determined to show that her defection was of no consequence.

Then as if a different decision had been made, the shutters were snapped open. His eyes darkened with a terrible intensity. They roved slowly over her face, engraving every detail of it on his memory. It was a look which held Cathy in thrall, unable to breathe or think. It squeezed her heart and sent little tremors of apprehension down her spine.

She could not look away even when Anthony clicked her glass with his. 'Let's drink a toast to ourselves,' he murmured close to her ear. 'To our future happiness together.'

Reacting automatically, Cathy picked up her glass. Tom's eyelids closed as if he had seen all he wished to see. He turned away, picked up his own glass and smiled at Vanessa. 'Good health!' he said, and drank deeply.

Cathy drank too—and shivered. That look in Tom's eyes . . . it had been like taking an imprint of her, a memory, a keepsake. Somehow she sensed that from now on she would no longer exist as a real person to him. She willed him to look at her again, just a glance to banish that awful impression, but he didn't. And all the happy emotions that Anthony's attentions had stirred slowly congealed into a heavy lump of lead.

CHAPTER EIGHT

THE light touch of fingertips on her thigh banished
all thoughts of Tom from Cathy's mind. The fingers
burrowed under the serviette on her lap, pulling the
silky material of her dress into little clusters, then
smoothing it back over the curve of her leg in a
movement so sensual that every muscle in her body
tensed.

Her mind jammed with horror. Not here! Anthony couldn't do it here! Not in front of his parents
and their closest friends. Oh no! she thought.
Carlton had only just passed behind them and was
now serving wine to the Rileys on Anthony's left. If
he looked back . . .

Cathy bit her lip to prevent it from trembling. So
many times in the past Anthony had embarrassed
her with his sly sexual manoeuvres while they were
in the company of others. He had answered her
protests by saying he could not help himself, that his
desire for her was all-consuming, that no one and
nothing else mattered. And in the name of love he
had bent her to his will. But he was not going to do it
to her here.

Conversations had started up around the table.
Tom was talking to Vanessa. Yet any sharp
movement might draw the attention Cathy so
desperately wanted to avoid. The fingers began a
slow stroking. The palm of Anthony's hand slid on to

her thigh, transmitting a heat which made her flesh crawl. The fingers swept upwards and inwards.

Calm ... she had to stay calm, not betray outwardly what was happening underneath the spotless white linen of a table napkin. Her skin prickled with fear. Her mind fixed a block-out of any sensations Anthony might arouse. She reached for her glass, bending forward, minimising any view of Anthony's action. She pressed her legs tightly together. Anthony's soft laughter burned in her ears.

To her intense relief the hand slid back until it was only lightly touching the outside of her leg. Anthony was half turned towards her and his whisper was husky with desire. 'Five years, Cathy. And my need for you has never left me.'

She turned to face eyes which were leaping with wild excitement. He could not be unaware of her fear or her panicky rejection of his action, yet as her eyes accused him, the excitement in his grew. Her heart contracted as memories screamed across her mind, memories that shame had carefully buried. Never would she tolerate his taking such liberties in public again, not in the name of love or desire or anything else.

Her eyes bit out the warning as she spoke with studied coolness. 'Don't think I'm the same malleable girl I was five years ago, Anthony. I told you then I didn't like it, and I still don't like it. If you won't respect my feelings about this, then you can't love me.'

There was a flicker of disbelief, a moment of utter stillness, then an inexplicable flare of elation as he removed his hand from all contact with her leg. 'I like that, Cathy,' he said with relish. 'You're all the more exciting for having grown into your own person.'

She searched his face, wanting to believe he spoke the truth. Until the offence of a few moments ago she had forgotten the torment of mind he had repeatedly inflicted with public intimacies. He had invariably laughed at what he called her prudery, just as he had laughed tonight. Would he really respect her wishes?

'Why did you do it? All those times in the past,' she demanded, needing an answer she could accept.

He shrugged and gave a whimsical smile. 'I wanted to. And you wanted it, Cathy.'

'No. I never did. And I told you so. It was unkind and cruel of you to force the issue past my objections.'

'Force?'

His voice held a note of quizzical surprise but there was no surprise in his eyes. A spark of amusement lurked in their green depths and Cathy had the disturbing impression that he was laughing inwardly.

'I never forced you into anything. Perhaps there were times when I pushed my own desires harder than you might have liked, but you did give in to them. You were willing, Cathy,' he reminded her pointedly.

Willing! It was probably the truth as he saw it, but Cathy could not help answering with bitter irony. 'What choice did I have? I had nothing left but you. If I displeased you, lost you . . . the price I had paid to be with you would have all been for nothing. And I couldn't face that.'

He frowned, apparently not carinq for her train of thought. 'What price?'

Her wry smile mocked his show of puzzlement. He knew, of course he knew. But she spelled it out. 'My family. The life which had been mine before you came along.'

'It was no life. And you were well rid of your family,' he said with arrogant dismissal.

Resentment burned into her eyes. 'You had a family to come back to, Anthony. And you did come back to them, back to all the comforts of Mirrima. There was no comfort for me, nothing to fall back on.'

His frown cut deeper this time. 'I thought . . .'

'Oh, yes—the mythical man who had taken over from you. Did you really believe I was likely to prefer some other man to you?'

He liked that. She saw the spark of triumph in his eyes before his expression gathered concern. 'You did change in those last couple of months, Cathy. Your whole attitude towards me changed.'

'Yes—Well, your parents saw to that, didn't they?'

'But now they've changed,' he said with strong emphasis. His face suddenly softened into winsome appeal. 'Do we have to hash over the past, Cathy? Haven't I done all I can to redress the situation? I love you. I want you to be happy.'

It checked the flow of bitterness, jolting her into recollecting herself. It was Anthony's hand on her leg that had opened the floodgates of the past. He was right in so far as the situation was different now. But did she love him?

The memories he had just evoked made her

wonder if she had ever really loved him in the past. Had it been her need for the open expression of love which had led her into a relationship with Anthony? And then, had she simply clung on to him because he had filled the vacuum created by her parents' rejection of her?

Mrs Elton came bustling in with the first course and Cathy was glad of the distraction. Nothing was simple. Love was not simple, life was not simple. She looked across at Tom and wished she could return to the uncomplicated tenor of her life a week ago, before Tom had declared his love, and before Anthony had come disrupting everything.

Tom was still chatting with Vanessa. Conversation remained divided into either end of the long table. No one seemed to have noticed the intensity of her interchange with Anthony. She realised that Anthony's possessive manner in the lounge-room would have given rise to an indulgence towards their excluding themselves from general conversation.

The soup was home-made pea and ham. Cathy ate automatically, barely registering the taste. The plates were removed by an Aboriginal girl, a frilly white apron over her neat black dress and a grin of absolute delight on her face. She had to be Jacko's sister, Lucy, Cathy decided. The grins were exactly the same. She wondered vaguely about their lives here at Mirrima, whether they were as uncomplicated as they seemed.

'Cathy.'

She turned warily to Anthony, all too conscious of the reserve which had clamped around her heart. He looked at her with the face of love. She did not know why she did not quite believe in his sincerity. He had been proving it to her, especially with his parents.

'Whatever I've done in the past, if it hurt you, it was done in ignorance. We were made for each other. If there's any question about that in your mind, I'll answer it tonight.'

Apprehension prickled down her spine. 'What do you mean, tonight?'

The answer was unmistakably written in his eyes even before he spoke, his voice lowered to an intense whisper. 'Later tonight I'll show you what love is. Why I love you, why you are the passion of my life. Will you let me fulfil every desire? Tell me yes. Tell me you want it as much as I do.'

Tonight! He wanted her tonight. Cathy's apprehension grew into sheer unreasoning panic. He would drive her to do things, turn her into a mindless slave to the sensuality he used so skilfully. She remembered nights when he had held her quivering on the edge of pain and ecstasy for hours, until she was almost crazy from it, a frenzied creature begging for release. But then he had been so loving afterwards, so loving she wuld weep from the intensity of her gratitude. He had drawn, executed, a total submission from her, possessing her mind as well as her body. Was that love?

'Why do you love me, Anthony?' she asked bluntly, driven by a need to settle the suspicion in her mind.

His smile was a provocative promise. 'I'll tell you later. Tonight.'

'I want to know now,' she persisted.

He laughed indulgently. 'You were always impatient! Anticipation is half the pleasure. Think about it, savour the thoughts.'

'No!' She faced him with rigid determination. 'Tell me why, Anthony.'

His eyes narrowed, measuring the strength of her will. He answered slowly but with absolute conviction. 'There are some people who call to one another, who answer needs in each other, an instinctive mating. That's us, Cathy. You, more than any other woman, have answered my needs. Give yourself to me, completely. Then you'll know that I love you.'

Sexual needs? Cathy frowned and turned away, her thoughts in more turmoil than ever. The second course arrived and was placed in front of her, lobster in a Mornay sauce. She heard Stephanie say that Anthony had brought fresh lobsters back from Sydney today. There were various comments made about seafood, but Cathy did not listen. She was considering Anthony's words, tasting them, chewing them over. She did not want to swallow them. She had not come back to Mirrima for a sexual replay of the past, she had come in search of her feelings for Anthony, and that involved a great deal more than the physical.

Yet the more she thought about it, the more she realised that the physical had dominated their relationship. She couldn't even remember their talking about anything but sex when they were alone. It was all they were talking about now. They had never had the kind of conversations she had enjoyed with Tom, discoursing on all manner of subjects.

The second course was cleared away and more wine was poured. Cathy looked across at Tom and saw him toss down the considerable quantity of wine left in his glass before Carlton arrived to refill it. She frowned over the uncharacteristic action. Tom was not an avid drinker—at least, he had only ever drunk sparingly whenever she had been out with him, enjoying the wine but not tossing it off as if it were water.

Vanessa murmured something to him. He smiled and began telling her a joke that Cathy had heard him tell before. Tom was a good raconteur. Mary Lachlan turned his way to listen in, then her husband leaned forward to catch what was being said. When the punch-line came they all laughed uproariously, drawing the attention of the rest of the table.

'Great joke!' boomed Ted Lachlan. 'Have you got any more up your sleeve, Tom?'

'Tell us another,' Vanessa urged gleefully.

He was persuaded. Everyone hung on his words and the whole table rocked with laughter at the end of his drily delivered tale. Cathy felt a surge of pride in Tom's ability to hold and entertain an audience. She was also glad to see him looking more relaxed. However, it disturbed her when he picked up his glass and poured its contents down his throat without a pause.

'Come on Tom. We won't let you stop now,' Carlton urged with hearty encouragement.

And indeed, everyone was looking at him with smiles of anticipation. Anthony started to say something to Cathy but she quickly hushed him into silence and ignored his frown of irritation. She wanted to listen to Tom.

His mouth held a slight curl as he began speaking, as if he were mocking himself for taking centre-stage or mocking the company for wanting it of him. He was not by nature an extrovert, never pushing himself forward unless he saw a necessity for it. Nevertheless, he rolled out a long, impossible story about a drunken man taking a shower with his clothes on, and laughter bubbled around the table at the amusing emphasis he gave to every absurdity.

His timing on each line was impeccable. He was brilliant, in better form than Cathy had ever heard him. Yet she gradually grew conscious of the slight pauses before words which needed care in their articulation, a slowness in his lip movements. She studied him more sharply, noting the slackness in his cheeks and heaviness in his eyelids. Shock rippled through her as understanding came. Tom was drunk.

No one else would notice the signs which were only visible to her because she knew him so well. He was containing his state of inebriation with almost faultless control, but Cathy's heart cringed. This was all her fault. He would never have drunk to this extent except to dull the pain she had inflicted.

In the general hilarity which followed his story Tom called for the decanter of wine. His glass was eagerly refilled with more pleas to continue the entertainment. The door from the kitchen opened and Mrs Elton wheeled in a traymobile loaded with dishes for the main course. Tom waved a limp hand towards it in a self-explanatory excuse for retirement.

Cathy thought she detected relief in the slight sag

of his face as he leaned back in his chair. His mouth curved down as he muttered to himself, '*La commedia è finita.*'

Cathy's heart sank. She knew the line. Tom had taken her to a performance of *I Pagliacci*. The tragic clown had carried on his role of giving amusement while his heart was breaking, and when he could bear it no longer he had retired with the words' The comedy is over'.

'What was that, Tom?' asked Vanessa in puzzled fashion.

He gave her a wry little smile. 'Just practising my Italian.'

'Are you planning a trip?'

He seemed to consider it for a moment then nodded. 'Yes. Yes, I'll be going to Italy, next week, in fact.'

Italy. Next week. Cathy's heart sank even lower. He was not only cutting her out of his life, he was going to cut all connection with her. Four years of cross-threads completely severed. Again she suffered the sense of brutal surgery, and Anthony's presence beside her did not defray one whit of the pain.

It disturbed her very deeply. If she truly loved Anthony, then surely Tom's leaving her should not hurt so much. Anthony's love should more than compensate for the loss. But right at this minute it didn't, it most certainly didn't. Maybe it would in time. She needed more time. But Anthony was pressing her now, tonight. She shook her head, postponing a decision once again.

Carlton carved the roast sirloin of beef. Mrs Elton handed steaming hot plates around while Lucy circulated with dishes of vegetables. The conversation over the meal revolved around food. Jim Partridge enquired of Carlton about the catering for tomorrow's crowd and both Carlton and Stephanie described the arrangements: barbecues, salads, beef and pork and lamb roasting on spits, and of course, kegs of beer and bars set up at all vantage points.

'Although there'll be about two hundred people milling around here by tomorrow night, you'll be the only important one, Cathy,' Anthony murmured. 'I'm going to see that it's the best day of your life.'

It drew a smile from her. Flattery it might be, but it was nice of him to make her feel so special. 'Won't you be needed for some duty or other with so many guests?'

He grinned. 'Some polite greeting when circumstances necessitate. I'll leave it to the parents. All the work details will be manned by the staff. Tomorrow is for fun and we're going to have it—swimming, riding, dancing . . .'

Cathy laughed and shook her head. 'No riding for me, Anthony. I didn't bring any clothes for it.'

'I'll get Van to lend you some. Remember the billabong where we picnicked the last time you were here?'

Picknicked and swam naked and made love under the trees . . . wild, desperate love, because she had known it was ending and didn't know how else to hold on. That was what Anthony was remembering, and what he wanted her to remember. But she found no joy in the memory.

The meal was cleared away. Bowls of artistically arranged fruit and platters of cheeses were set around the table. A sweet white wine was served, and Cathy glanced anxiously at Tom, who was once again wasting no time in tasting it.

'Do you still do any rowing, Tom?'

Stephanie's question surprised Cathy and she was curious to hear Tom's answer. He had never spoken about rowing to her, but now that the point had been brought up, she realised he was certainly built like a rower with his massive shoulders and muscular arms.

He shook his head and his reply was completely uninterested. 'No. I gave it up years ago, Stephanie.'

'What a shame! You were so good at it. Your father showed me all your trophies and the photographs of your victories.'

'What victories?' Vanessa asked eagerly.

Cathy sensed Anthony's irritation at her own switch of attention on to Tom but she wanted to hear the answer to Vanessa's question.

Tom smiled a smile which was a million miles away, a secret, introspective smile that no one else would understand except Cathy, and it twisted her heart. She remembered how she had felt when Anthony had chosen Mirrima instead of her five years ago. Nothing else had mattered. No achievement in her life had meant a damn; it was all ashes.

Stephanie supplied the answer. 'Tom stroked the Monash University Eight to second place in the Victorian Championships.'

Cathy thought how ironic it was that Stephanie Pryor-Jones should know something about Tom's life that she herself did not. She had been too self-absorbed to ask Tom for information which did not concern her directly. An emotional cripple, he had called her. Had Anthony done that to her, driving her so far into herself that she had lost the desire to involve herself with others?

'Cathy did better than that,' drawled Anthony, and the one-upmanship in his tone made Cathy cringe. 'At fifteen she was a New South Wales swimming champion,' he boasted for her. 'Four-hundred-metre medley. You should have seen her cleave through the water! It was beautiful to watch.'

Cathy's cheeks scorched with embarrassment as she became the focus of attention.

'You knew Cathy when she was fifteen, Anthony?' Mary Lachlan asked interestedly.

'No. Cathy was seventeen when she first bewitched me, Mary,' he said, casting an intimate little smile at Cathy. 'But she was still training at that time—a gruelling schedule. Two hours in the pool before she went off to a day's work and two more hours after it. Five hours on Saturday and Sunday, with her father standing over her like a martinet. The man was heartless, pushing her to do better all the time, refusing to recognise that enough was enough. Hungry for reflected glory, never mind what his daughter wanted. Isn't that so, Cathy?'

The heat in Cathy's cheeks burned even more painfully. It wasn't true of her father, not the reflected glory part, or the pushing. He had simply practised what he believed, that any God-given talent should be used to the full. 'I didn't mind, Anthony. My father only did what he thought was best for me,' she said quietly, hoping he would drop this line of conversation.

'The cruelties we parents inflict on our children without being aware of it!' Myra Partridge commented reflectively, then shot a sympathetic smile at Cathy. 'But I do commend you for your loyalty, my dear.'

'Must have been hard, all those hours' training,' Bill Curran remarked.

'It was monstrous,' Anthony declared emphatically. 'Cathy wasn't allowed any normal life at all. No dates, no fun—church on Sunday was her only outing. Best thing I ever did was to rescue her from all that and see that she experienced another side of life. And look at her now. She's gone from success to success, haven't you, darling? I'm so proud of her.'

Cathy inwardly winced at the endearment, spoken right out in front of Tom. And she fiercely resented Anthony's taking credit for her success. It was Tom who had helped her and stood by her—although some credit was due to Anthony, she thought with grim irony. He had been the destructive force which had inadvertently fired her ambition.

'In fact, the last year I had in Armidale with Cathy was the happiest year of my life. She's an incredible woman,' Anthony burbled on with growing relish for his subject, 'and I bet it's been the same for Tom these last few years that Cathy's been in Sydney, because you've been such good friends. What do you say, Tom?'

The blood drained from Cathy's face. At that moment she could have killed Anthony. She rose instantly to Tom's defence in a frantic attempt to prevent Anthony from torturing him further.

'For my part, my years in Sydney have given me

more satisfaction and contentment than any other period of my life,' she stated flatly, and shot a look of apologetic appeal to Tom.

His eyes were on Anthony and they were no longer dull or opaque. They held a dangerous glitter. Cathy tensed and glanced sharply at Anthony. His eyes were also glittering and there was a little curl of amusement on his mouth. Cathy's brain screamed in protest. Why? Why was he taunting Tom? Then she remembered Anthony's irritation when she had switched her attention from him to Tom. Jealousy? A need to hit off Tom and prove himself the better man? It was so mean! Mean and petty and cruel!

'I am surprised that, having seen Mirrima, Cathy could have been contented anywhere else,' Tom said smoothly, his measured tone holding no hint of the underlying dig at both Cathy and Anthony. He turned his face to Carlton. 'You have the most beautiful property it's ever been my privilege to see, and I thank you and Stephanie for so graciously receiving me as your guest.'

He pushed back his chair and rose to his feet, giving a suggestion of a bow to Stephanie. 'You're a wonderful hostess, Stephanie. I've indulged myself with great food and wine tonight, and enjoyed the good company of your friends.' He swept the table with a smile. 'But I think I'll be in better condition to enjoy tomorrow if I seek my bed now. So, if you'll excuse me . . .'

The dry humour in this last speech evoked several chuckles from the men.

'Oh, Tom! Do you have to go?' Vanessa wailed appealingly.

'I'm afraid I must.'

'I'm sorry you're leaving us early, Tom,' Stephanie said, adding with the graciousness of a great hostess, 'but we'll all look forward to your company tomorrow.'

'Hear, hear!' Ted Lachlan heartily agreed. 'Sleep well, Tom.'

A chorus of goodnights and a wave of goodwill followed him out of the dining-room. Cathy stared after him, almost bursting with admiration. She had always liked and respected Tom, but never had she liked and respected and admired him so much as she did at this moment. All evening he had conducted himself superbly well, under the most difficult of circumstances, and when, at the end of it, Anthony had provoked an intolerable situation, Tom had defused it with charm and dignity.

He was a man whom anyone would be proud to call a friend, and Cathy mourned the loss of his friendship. Suddenly she could not bear to remain at the dinner-party either. She stood up and fixed a smile on her face.

'If you don't mind, Stephanie, I think I'll follow Tom's example. It's been a long day and I'm very tired. Thank you so much, and goodnight to you all.'

'I'll see you to your door, Cathy,' Anthony said quickly, rising to his feet and moving her chair back for an easy departure.

So angry did she feel with him that it was on the tip of Cathy's tongue to refuse his offer. However, second thoughts persuaded her to accept without comment. She wanted a private talk with Anthony. She was in the fighting mood to say a few pertinent

words. And none of them had anything whatsoever
to do with sex!

CHAPTER NINE

CATHY'S heart was thumping hard as she mounted the stairs with Anthony. The hand on her elbow had slid to her waist and she did not have to look at him to know what was on his mind. She hurried her step, angered by his assumption as well as his treatment of Tom. She would let Anthony into her bedroom, but certainly not into her bed. As soon as he paused to close the door behind them she whirled out of his grasp and put several steps of distance between them before turning to face him, eyes blazing.

'How could you do that to Tom? Have you no sensitivity at all? Did you have to twist the knife? Isn't it enough that I . . .'

'Now just hold on a minute,' Anthony broke in, his face a study of injured innocence. 'What am I supposed to have done?'

Cathy seethed at the pretence. 'First you put him down about the rowing, which he didn't even bring into the conversation. And then . . . then you tried to score off him by making his relationship with me of less importance than what I had with you. He's suffered enough without your . . .'

'Suffered? Come on, Cathy! Did Tom look as if he was suffering tonight? He latched on to Vanessa without a backward glance at you and then he was the life and soul of the party.'

'Anthony, you know better than that! You were

115

with me this afternoon.'

'Yes, and I saw a man whose pride was wounded. Nothing more. Now, if all you want to do is discuss Tom, go and discuss it with him. I'm not interested in the subject. My only interest is in us, you and me.'

The selfishness of his challenge only hardened Cathy's heart against him. Her belligerent stance did not waver.

It was Anthony who softened. He gave a sigh of exasperation, then gestured appeasement as he gentled his voice. 'All right, you feel sorry for him. But I feel jealous of the years he had with you. Let's get this into perspective. You came to Mirrima for me, not for Tom.'

Some of the stiffening seeped out of her spine, and she eyed him with slightly less acrimony. 'That's not entirely correct. I came back to Mirrima to find the truth.'

Anthony shrugged. 'What's truth? It depends on your point of view.'

'Maybe,' she admitted testily. 'But I'm only just beginning to look, Anthony. I buried what we had five years ago; it was too painful to remember. But you forced me to remember last night, and now I'm starting to see it as it was. I thought Mirrima was the heart of the problem . . . your parents, the style of life you had been born to, the difference in our backgrounds. But now I'm beginning to understand that it was not all of the problem, nor even the most important part.'

Anthony threw up his hands in impatience. 'All this philosophy! I can't even pretend to follow what you're saying. We're just wasting a lot of time talking.'

'That's right!' Cathy bit back. 'You never did want to talk, Anthony.'

He suddenly grinned. 'No, I never did with you. Not when we were in a bedroom together. You look magnificent when you're angry, Cathy. Eyes sparking blue fire, every line of your body taut with emotion!'

She spun away from him and walked over to the window, hating the way her pulse had quickened at his words. She looked out over a moon-drenched Mirrima and knew she felt more mixed up than ever. She had felt so strongly about Tom at the table, she hadn't cared about Anthony's feelings at all, and yet there was this physical thing he could tug at will. Was it the memory of intimacy or was it something more immediate, an instinctive mating as he claimed?

His hands slid around her waist and he pulled her body back against his. A little shudder ran through her, but she felt too tired to resist. His mouth brushed her hair and his breath near her ear was a warm sigh.

'There was always something better to do, my love. A better way to talk. If you'll . . .'

She tensed. 'Don't ask me now, Anthony. Please, just leave it tonight. I want you to go and I want to go to bed alone.'

'You're not going to sleep in the state you're in. You're far too tense, seething with emotion. And it's all so simple, Cathy. Relax, lean back against me, let me soothe you.' His hands moved up to cup her breasts.

'No! I don't want you to touch me like that,' she cried in panic, trying to pluck his hands away.

His thumbs moved across her nipples, back and forth, back and forth, and she shivered as they hardened under his touch.

'Your body is giving me another answer, and that's where the truth lies, Cathy. I'm your first lover and for the rest of your life you'll never be able to forget how I touched you, and how you responded. Those memories will never be erased. After what we had, anything else will only be second best or third best or worse. That's why you came back to Mirrima.'

His lips were on her ear, tantalising with little nibbles as he spoke. Then his mouth trailed down her throat and without any conscious will of her own Cathy moved her head to one side, giving way to him.

'Remember how it was the first time with us,' he murmured huskily, 'slowly discovering each other. I've never felt such tenderness with a woman as I did with you that day. That's what I'm feeling now. I want to capture that again with you, forget the years and start anew—a better start, even more beautiful, because what will follow will be better.'

She wanted to. It had been beautiful the first time. He had been loving, tender, soothing her fears with a gentleness which had won her acquiescence. But she had been so innocent then; she had believed him, trusted him. She no longer had that innocence or that trust, and the insistent worms of doubt overrode the melting weakness inside her. She dragged in a determined breath, forced Anthony's hands down and swung around to face him.

'Don't pressure me, Anthony. I'll tell you when I'm ready to go to bed with you, if and when I'm ever ready. It's not tonight.'

His eyes challenged hers for a long moment, burning desire meeting steely defiance to no visible effect. His mouth twitched into a reluctant smile of admiration, then, to Cathy's astonishment, he threw back his head and laughed. It was a laugh of triumph, of joyous satisfaction, and even when he stopped laughing, the green eyes danced delight at her.

'Not tonight,' he rolled back at her in twinkling appreciation. Then with a strange fervour of approval, 'Ah, Cathy, you truly are a prize amongst women! You always were the ultimate challenge and you're still the same . . . teasingly beautiful, endlessly provocative, the eternal temptress just one step out of reach. You're right to do it. It makes the final consummation so much more exciting.'

He tilted her chin and ran the tip of his tongue across her lips. 'Tomorrow I'll taste all of you,' he breathed, and Cathy could sense his mounting excitement. 'You'll come to me, just as you always did, because you can't stay away.' And on that exultant claim he left, casting a last simmering look at her as he shut the door.

Cathy stood rooted to the spot, her heart thudding a painful protest as her mind groped towards thoughts which cut into the past, rearranging it, shaping it into something so different that Cathy was frightened to look at it. But she had to. That was why she had come to Mirrima, to sort out the past and discover her true feelings.

The ultimate challenge: she had never meant to challenge Anthony, yet that was how he thought of her. Why? The prize amongst women; the prize because she was the hardest to get? With Anthony's looks and wealth and charm, he surely found little problem in getting any girl he wanted, but there had been almost insurmountable barriers to forming a relationship with her, breaking down the religious beliefs which had been instilled in her from childhood, undermining the desire to keep on with her swimming training, alienating her from a family which forbade boy-girl relationships outside the church group.

There had been no one the least bit attractive to Cathy in the church group, and Anthony had given her something she had never known ... the pleasure of finding herself attractive to a man of so many attractions, the excitement of being wanted, being loved, being told that Anthony's whole life revolved around seeing her, being with her. The temptation to accept his invitations had grown over months of persistent and very flattering persuasion until she could no longer resist, despite the hateful necessity of deceiving her parents.

Yet as much as she was drawn by the love Anthony promised, her sense of guilt had denied his desire to make love to her for much longer than he had probably experienced with other girls. Maybe she had been the ultimate challenge. Her surrender had finally been won by his passionate declaration that he could no longer bear to keep seeing her, that her rejection of his love was destroying him.

Anthony had made that first lovemaking beautiful.

It had seemed right, until he had taken her home. Cathy closed her eyes as that terrible scene flooded back into her memory. She had agreed to Anthony's meeting her parents, hoping that he could persuade them that his regard for her was sincere and their relationship should be approved. But far from being tactful, Anthony had revealed everything, showering contempt on all the principles by which her family lived. Her father had reacted with violent righteousness, ejecting them both from the family home with such an outpouring of vituperation that Cathy had been too dazed by shock to know what to do.

She had needed Anthony's love then, above everything else. If she had not believed in it, and believed in her love for him, then the wreckage of all she had known would have been unbearable. But had it been love or need which had made her cling to Anthony?

In complete mental turmoil Cathy started to dredge out more memories. Had Anthony ever really cared about her feelings? He had demanded submission from her, in everything. When she did not immediately give it, his love, on which she so desperately depended, was abruptly withdrawn. He had made her do things or accept things she instinctively shrank from, like the public sexual stimulation he had tried tonight.

Anthony was a taker. The realisation jolted her all the more because Tom had recognised it so quickly. And Tom was a giver. Right from their first meeting Tom had been giving her whatever she needed, and

she had accepted, with all too little regard for him
and his feelings. For four years she had been a taker,
just like Anthony, and the thought made her writhe
in shame.

Sick from a churning mêlée of emotions, Cathy
undressed, pulled on her nightdress and trudged into
the bathroom. She washed her face clean of make-up
and stared at her pallid reflection in the vanity
mirror. It was not the face of a beautiful, teasing
temptress; she was more and more inclined to think
it was the face of a blind, stupid fool. She turned
away, switched off the lights and climbed into the
four-poster bed, the bed Anthony had chosen for her,
expecting her to share it with him, making love.

Had it ever really been love? She remembered the
anxiety which had threaded through her need for
him, always living with the threat hanging over her
head that their relationship was at risk because he
kept demanding more and more proof of her love,
until she did all that he required of her, too confused
to know right from wrong, or what she really felt
about him. Anthony, always ths master, always
winning, always getting what he wanted.

In the end it had been total submission. When he
made love to her he even compelled her to lie
passively beneath him, only moving at his command, and the more passive she was the more
excited he was. Every instinct had told her it was
wrong, and yet she had taken reassurance from it,
believing that she was indispensable to him. And she
had needed him, too much to question anything.

Cathy shuddered and pulled the bedclothes more
closely around her. She had not been indispensable.

The love she had needed so badly had been completely cut off. Because of his parents, Mirrima . . . or because she had submitted to everything Anthony had wanted, and she was no longer a challenge for him? Five years ago she could not have faced the idea that Anthony had not really loved her. Nor could she have thought for one moment that she had not loved him. Even now the conclusions she was reaching made her feel sick. But were they true?

One thing was certain: she was not going to submit to any sexual advances from Anthony this weekend, or until she truly wanted them. Tom had loved her for years without thrusting sexual demands upon her. She had never said no to him. Somehow he had known, sensed that she couldn't cope with that kind of pressure. If Anthony really loved her he could wait too, like Tom.

And her feelings for Tom—that was another thing. She had been a blind fool there, hurting him, badly. She could not leave the situation as it was. Somehow she had to repair the damage that had been done, as best she could. Make him see that she now felt differently. She was no longer an emotional cripple who could be bent to anyone's will.

She groaned and buried her face in the pillow. She could not bear the thought of losing Tom, losing his respect, his support, his love. She wasn't sure why it meant so much to her, but it did. If he left her, went to Italy . . . The full dimensions of the hole he would leave in her life were suddenly too awful to contemplate. She had to stop him.

And despite all the heart and mind-searching she had given to Anthony, as Cathy drifted into sleep, there was only the one thought which kept pounding through her brain. It was terribly, terribly important that she keep Tom in her life.

CHAPTER TEN

CATHY struggled out of another disturbing dream and forced her eyelids open. Relief washed through her. It was light; the long, wretched night was over. She shrugged off the vague torment of formless nightmares which had punctuated her restless sleep and sharpened her thoughts to the day ahead of her.

A darted glance at the clock told her it was almost seven, time to get moving. The last thing she wanted was a good-morning call from Anthony while she was still in her nightdress, or in the process of getting dressed. She was not a teasing temptress and had no intention of giving any excuse for such an accusation. Anthony would have to face that truth and accept what she had decided, or their relationship could not develop into what she wanted.

The conclusions she had drawn last night might be right or wrong; Anthony could very well have changed since she last knew him. But one thing had certainly changed. She was no longer the pliant creature Anthony had known before. She had changed and forged a will of her own, thanks to Tom.

Her mind slid over the problem of Tom. That was still too painful to think about. She knew she had to breach the wall he had put between them some time today, but not this morning. If he was hung over from last night's indulgence he would be in no mood

125

to indulge her. Besides, she needed to clarify her mind about Anthony first.

With a new-found sense of purpose, Cathy threw the bedclothes aside and swung her legs to the floor. Some twenty minutes later she was out of her room and while she felt a certain amount of relief at avoiding another bedroom encounter with Anthony, she could not repress a growing sense of apprehension as she made her way downstairs. How was Anthony going to react to her hold-off attitude?

Mrs Elton was in the great hall, wheeling a hostess cart towards the verandah. The housekeeper paused and smiled at Cathy. 'Breakfast on the . . . Oh, of course you know that, dear. Sleep well?'

'Yes, thank you, Mrs Elton,' Cathy lied.

The friendly eyes crinkled in pleased approval as they took in the pink T-shirt with the patchwork trim, the full, peasant style of the patchwork skirt, and the pink loafers on Cathy's feet. 'Well, you do look lovely, Miss Cathy. But to my old eyes you always did. I do hope you have a good time.'

Cathy returned the smile and thanked her again. A good time was probably beyond the realms of possibility, considering all that had happened, but she had dressed herself to boost her confidence and she was pleased to have the housekeeper's approval. She moved quickly ahead to open the doors for the dear old woman.

The verandah ran the whole length of this northern side of the house. Being some six metres wide, it provided a huge entertainment area, as well as casual accommodation. It was completely screened to keep out unwelcome insects, and by tonight its floor would be covered by foldaway stretchers for the children of the incoming guests. Adults would be bunking down anywhere—in their vehicles, the woolshed, the summerhouse by the pool—and as Carlton had declared last night, some considerable number would not be bothered about sleeping at all.

Anthony was not at the breakfast table, neither were Tom or Vanessa. All the others from last night's party were present, except for Carlton. Everyone greeted Cathy with an air of welcoming pleasure and she found herself responding without any awkwardness. It was so easy to fit in when she was accepted as 'one of them'. They weren't bad people, not even Stephanie; they were simply bred to a station of life which disdained anything lower.

'I didn't expect to see you down so soon,' Stephanie said warmly, 'and neither did Anthony. I'm afraid he's gone off on an early morning ride.'

Cathy's inner tension eased a little. She had time to overcome the apprehension she felt. She took herself in hand. There was no need to feel apprehensive. She had every right to expect Anthony to respect her feelings. She was not a doormat for him to walk over as he pleased.

Stephanie smiled at the housekeeper. 'Thanks, Doris. You've arrived just at the right time and that should do our young people.' She waved Cathy to the hostess cart. 'Help yourself to whatever you'd like and take a chair—no formality today. Carlton's gone to do the rounds, and Vanessa and Tom aren't down yet.'

Cathy hoped that Tom would stay in bed while she

had breakfast. She knew she had to face him sooner or later today, but she was not at all sure how she would cope with the feelings his presence would inevitably arouse. She looked at the dishes of bacon and eggs, felt an instant revulsion to food of any kind, then hurriedly took some toast, poured herself a cup of coffee, and sat down next to Mary Lachlan.

The conversation around the table picked up again. Cathy half listened to it as she forced herself to eat. Mostly it referred to people she did not know and she was not required to make any contribution to the general chat.

She had almost finished her meagre breakfast when Anthony breezed on to the verandah, coming to an abrupt halt when he saw her at the table. He looked strikingly handsome in his riding-clothes; the living, breathing picture of virility, shirt lying open to halfway down his broad, tanned chest, jodhpurs moulding the muscular calves of his legs, riding boots adding more inches to his impressive height. All he needed was a riding-whip to complete the image of aggressive male dominance.

But Cathy did not want to be dominated, at least not in the way Anthony had dominated her in the past. On the other hand, she had to acknowledge the sheer physical impact which was so much part of the man. On the surface he would be attractive to any woman, irresistible to a seventeen-year-old innocent. She could forgive herself that first, long-ago surrender.

Anthony's delight on seeing her was mingled with a slight grimace of frustration. 'Down already? I was going to give myself the pleasure of waking you up,' he remarked, in careless disregard for the interpretation that anyone at the table could put to his words.

Cathy prickled with resentment. 'Good morning,' she said coolly.

He grinned as he walked towards her. 'It's a great morning. I'm going to show it to you once I've changed and breakfasted.'

His hand slid around the nape of her neck in a slow, deliberate caress. Somehow it seemed to denote an ownership which Cathy instinctively rejected. She arched forward, away from his disturbing touch.

He seemed to disregard the movement. 'Sleep well?' he asked easily.

'Very comfortably,' she asserted firmly, hoping Anthony could see no signs of her restless night. He would probably put it down to sexual frustration, which couldn't be further from the truth.

He laughed and turned away. 'Don't move. I'll have a quick shower and be with you again in a few minutes.'

Vanessa came down while he was still absent. Tom was not with her, a fact which afforded Cathy some considerable relief. That relief surprised her, and she examined it. She knew Vanessa was interested in Tom, certainly interested enough to have wanted his company at breakfast. If Tom had given the girl any encouragement at all, surely she would have tried to get him out of bed early this morning so that he could be with her every possible minute.

Therefore Tom had not encouraged her, Tom was not interested. Cathy realised that she didn't want him to be interested in Vanessa. She felt a strong sense of possessiveness about him which rather shocked her. It was so terribly selfish under the circumstances, but she could not dismiss it.

The desultory conversation around the table ceased as Anthony sauntered back in, dressed now in form-fitting blue jeans and an emerald-green sports-shirt which added lustre to his eyes. 'I don't think I've ever seen Mirrima look so beautiful as it does this morning,' he declared with pride. 'I'm going to show you all over it, Cathy.'

'Anthony, that would take all day!' Stephanie expostulated as he moved to the hostess cart. 'Our guests will start arriving in an hour or so.'

'I won't be needed. You and Dad and Vanessa can put out the welcome mat,' he tossed at her carelessly, and heaped a pile of bacon and eggs and toast on a plate.

Stephanie was vexed. 'Anthony, there are people coming who will want to see you.'

'Then they can wait upon my convenience.'

Cathy found herself in sympathy with Anthony's mother. He was doing it again, riding roughshod over others' feelings, only considering his own. 'Don't I have any say in it?' she asked sharply.

Stephanie half jumped in her seat and cast a half-apprehensive glance at Anthony. 'Yes, of course,' she rattled out quickly. 'You two do whatever pleases you. Enjoy yourselves.'

Anthony turned around with a triumphant smile and Cathy smothered a sigh. Apparently Anthony had come down so heavily on his mother yesterday that she was not game to suggest that Cathy should not have prime consideration, or that there was anything more important for Anthony to do than giving her pleasure.

'In that case, we might have a look at the home paddocks,' Cathy stated slowly. It suited her purpose to be alone with Anthony for a while, to clear the air and find out more about her feelings before she had to see Tom. 'But we'll be back in an hour to help you with your guests, Stephanie, I promise.'

Ted Lachlan chuckled. 'Love always finds a way,' he said teasingly, and all the faces around the table reflected his indulgent amusement.

Inwardly Cathy cringed, but she fixed a non-committal smile on her face.

Anthony threw her a mocking look. 'Compromises never satisfy either party—you should know that by now, Cathy.'

Only she had not compromised. She was doing exactly as she wished. And she was not going to compromise with Anthony either.

Everyone started discussing the forthcoming invasion of guests and the general agenda for the day's entertainment. Anthony ate his meal with a hearty appetite, ignoring the conversation. He had eyes only for Cathy and the expression in those green eyes held a hunger that food wasn't satisfying. Cathy held on to her determination. She was not going to feed his sexual appetite.

As soon as he had finished eating, Anthony blithely excused both of them from the table and led Cathy outside. He took a deep breath and sighed his satisfaction. 'Nothing like an early morning ride to clear the brain of cobwebs and invigorate the body.

You'll have to come with me in future, Cathy, often. On horseback—cars aren't half as good.'

They were walking towards the old coach-house where the farm vehicles were garaged. 'How far into the future are you looking?' Cathy asked bluntly. He had talked about the future five years ago, a future which had never come.

He laughed and gave her a knowing grin which was no answer at all. Once in the coach-house he steered her towards a Range Rover and helped her into the high cabin of the four-wheel drive. He climbed into the driver's seat and started the engine before speaking again.

'If we've only got an hour, we'd better get moving fast. There's a lot to see and a lot to do.' His smile was all too suggestive. 'Perhaps we can stretch that time a bit. Nobody will notice, nobody will care.' He was cocky, full of bubbly cheer, on top of the world, and he drove the Range Rover out of the coach-house with exuberant acceleration.

'No, Anthony. I said an hour and that's what it's going to be,' Cathy insisted firmly. 'We're not stretching anything. We're going to come back and you're going to do the decent thing by greeting the guests with the rest of your family.'

He glanced across at her, his eyes sparkling devilment. 'You're irresistible when you look determined! Give me a kiss.'

If she gave him a challenge, he asked for submission, Cathy noted grimly, but she did not submit. 'You're driving, Anthony.'

He leaned towards her. 'So?'

'Watch where you're going.'

'There's not a fence for miles. Besides, I can always stop the car. I want you to kiss me.' His gaze remained on her, commandingly intense.

Agitated by his reckless disregard of the moving vehicle, Cathy almost gave in, just to get his attention back on driving. Then her spine stiffened. This was precisely the type of pressure Anthony had practised on her in the past. 'No!' she said fiercely. 'You said you were going to show me Mirrima, so show it to me.'

He chuckled and settled back in his seat. 'You're right—everything in its place. I love this land of ours. I doubt there's another property in the world to equal it.'

Cathy was rather bemused by the quick change in him. However, as he spoke on about Mirrima she began to realise the full depth of his commitment to it. There was no doubt that it was the ruling passion of his life.

He drove down by the river flats where kilometre after kilometre of tall, lush green lucerne stretched as far as the eye could see. 'We put permanent irrigation in here three years ago, doubled the area we could crop and tripled the yield,' he said proudly. 'I'll show you the experimental paddocks. New, fast-growing, rust-resistant wheat—the most impressive crop we ve ever had. It's a great sight.'

It was too. Anthony stopped the vehicle and drank it in with a deeper appreciation than Cathy could ever have. 'Look at it. It's the most valuable thing we have, land like this. The future of the world depends on sixteen centimetres of top-soil. And we have the best.'

His pride was so evident. Anthony was too involved in the wonder of Mirrima to be receptive to a change of subject, and Cathy wondered how she was going to introduce what was on her mind.

They drove slowly over Brokenback Ridge, Anthony talking all the time, pointing out the flocks of sheep in the northern pastures. 'A grand season. We've never carried so many sheep to the hectare and they still haven't grazed it down.'

He rambled on. Cathy was only half listening. Time was running out. Anthony drove up to the top of Mount Mirral, the one unproductive area on Mirrima, but the point from which much of the property near the homestead could be seen. The view was breathtaking. Anthony stopped the Range Rover and sat back with a sigh of contentment, lord and master of all he surveyed.

The thought came to Cathy in a swift stab of terrible sadness, and before she could choke it off, it tumbled into words. 'If you had ever loved me as much as you do Mirrima, all that misery would never have been.'

That was the truth, and it had been spoken. The words hovered in the silence which followed, an unnaturally still silence. Cathy could not bring herself to look at Anthony's face. She saw his hands tighten their grip on the steering-wheel, knuckles whitening. If he lied to her now, then everything would have been a lie.

'Cathy.' His voice was strained, as if struggling past barriers which had been in place for so long, they were difficult to circumvent. 'You're right!' It was an explosion of intense emotion. 'I've loved

Mirrima from the time I was born. It possesses me as much as I possess it and I couldn't live without it.'

Then hesitantly, 'I know there was no other man in your life, back then. I don't want to hurt you. I can only tell you this because that time is past. I thought you were everything I wanted in a woman. You satisfied all the needs in me which had never been satisfied before. But when I brought you here you didn't fit, not for Mirrima. It wasn't your fault, but you . . . it doesn't matter now.'

His voice broke into vehement passion as he spoke on. 'You do now—that's the important thing. You'd fit anywhere. Mirrima is one of the greatest, the most precious things in the world to me. And you're the other, Cathy. You're right for it now. That's the truth: you're right for it now. Even my parents see it.'

A cold knife twisted in her heart. She had been right—almost. Anthony had not loved her. Her eyes filled with tears as sadness engulfed her, a silent mourning for a dream which had always been false.

'It's yours now, Cathy,' he continued with growing fervour. 'I'm laying it at your feet. I brought you here on purpose to see it. Mistress of it all, Cathy, by my side, together. I know I hurt you, I know I haven't been fair. But I'm making all the reparation I can. I want you to share all of it with me now.'

Promises. False promises? Yet for the first time in his life he was being honest with her, as he saw it. He turned to her and even through the blur of her tears she could see the deep yearning in his eyes, and was touched by it. His face suddenly softened with an expression of great tenderness.

'I love you, Cathy. Don't cry, my darling. We have

the future.'

And before Cathy could do anything about it, he leaned over and pressed his mouth to hers. It was not a kiss of passion, nor even of sensual persuasion; it was a kiss of homage, of reverence, like the first time he had kissed her so long ago. And just as then, Cathy's lips trembled under his, and she felt faint from the rush of emotion that swirled through her. The first kiss and the last, and all that had been in between, finished. And this was the only memory she would keep, the only one worth keeping.

Anthony drew back a little and a quirky little smile curved his lips. His eyes held a sardonic bemusement. 'You make me do things that even surprise me! Let's get out and make love, up here, with Mirrima spread out beneath us.'

'No,' she whispered, too choked by the weight of all her memories to speak more firmly. Her eyes swept over the vista he offered. Mirrima had corrupted Anthony, his parents, Vanessa. It would probably corrupt anyone. Too much wealth. It was enough to make anyone lose sight of the value of people.

He reached for her, dragged her into his arms. She automatically strained away from his embrace and her eyes flew to his in angry protest. It wasn't tenderness that looked back at her but a burning desire which mocked her reluctance.

'I want you, Cathy, and I want you now,' he said with a touch of ruthlessness which sent a shiver down her spine.

'No.' Her eyes threw back a stony denial.

A glitter of excitement entered his. 'Do you want

me to force you?'

She swallowed down the frightened lump in her throat and spoke as calmly and forcefully as she could. 'No, I don't want you to force me. That would be rape, because I don't want to make love with you. Never again. It's over, what there was between us. I don't want any more of it.'

His face tightened and his eyes narrowed in hard concentration on her. 'You're teasing!'

'I'm not teasing.'

A grimness settled around his mouth. 'You can't do this to me, Cathy.'

'Yes, I can,' she retorted determinedly.

'So this is what I get for telling the truth!' he grated, his tone harsh and accusing, his hands sliding to her arms, fingers biting into her flesh. 'You're paying me back for what I did five years ago.' He suddenly let her go, tossing her back against her door. He turned away from her in savage disgust and thumped the wheel with the flat of his hand. 'God— a man's a fool ever to tell a woman the truth!'

He sliced her a look of furious frustration. 'You'll pay for this, Cathy. Don't think I'll go without while you get around to changing your mind!'

The threat, just the same as it had always been, only it had no force for Cathy now. She felt too sick and shaken to answer it. The truth she had suspected last night had been confirmed.

Anthony switched on the engine and revved it to an unholy roar. 'Enjoy your sulk!' he shouted at her. 'You'll regret it soon enough!'

The trip back to the homestead was a jolting nightmare, but Cathy did not care. The faster the

better. There was no more to be said. She did not love
Anthony. She suspected she never had, but that did
not matter any more. The past could finally be laid to
rest, permanently. Nothing mattered now but
getting back to Tom, who did value people.

As soon as the Range Rover came to a screeching
halt, she was out, not waiting for Anthony in his
raging temper to do anything for her. He caught her
just outside the coach-house and spun her around to
him. His eyes were a blaze of aggression.

'Don't try me too far, Cathy. Nobody toys with
me!'

She was still shaky from the bumpy ride he had
just given her, and anger at his arrogant assumption
sharpened her voice. 'Just let me go, Anthony. I
don't want anything from you.

He wasn't going to let her go. She could see the
need to dominate crystallising in the green eyes,
becoming harder, ruthless in purpose.

'Hey, Anthony! We're here!'

The shout distracted him. A station-wagon was
making a slow approach along the driveway to the
house, a girl half hanging out of the back passenger
window.

It halted, and the girl thrust her door open, jumped
out, then waved the other occupants on. It took
Cathy only a moment to recognise who she was:
Jillian Barnsworth, Anthony's companion at the
ball, and she was flying across the lawn towards
them.

Anthony's gaze returned sharply to Cathy, raking
her with fierce frustration. 'Jillian would beg for
what you're refusing.'

'And you'd make her beg, wouldn't you?' Cathy whipped back with venom. Her chin lifted in proud defiance. 'Jillian is welcome to you. I don't care what you do.'

His eyes glinted with dangerous fire. 'You care, Cathy. And I'll make you know it before this day's out. You'll change your mind, my love,' he grated savagely before stepping back from her and holding out his arms to Jillian.

The girl flew into them, hugging him with uninhibited fervour. Anthony's eyes flashed a vengeful challenge at Cathy before he recomposed his face to smiling indulgence.

'Well, hi to you too, sweetheart,' he purred.

'Oh, Anthony! I'd thought we'd never get here. It was bad enough having to go home with Mum and Dad yesterday, but Dad was ambling along this morning like a hundred-year-old snail.' Jillian belatedly slewed around to acknowledge Cathy, but one arm still lay claim to Anthony's waist and her eyes were triumphant with her sense of possession. 'Hello. Cathy, isn't it? We met at the ball.'

'Yes, we did,' Cathy agreed softly, feeling a wave of sympathy for the girl. With her long brown hair hanging free and dressed in tightly fitting jeans and T-shirt, Jillian looked even younger than she had at the ball, all too vulnerable to a man like Anthony, just as Cathy herself had been so long ago.

'Well, you'd better take me around the front of the house to greet your parents,' suggested Anthony, giving her an affectionate squeeze. His eyes mocked Cathy over Jillian's head and without another word to her he turned aside and strolled off with Jillian.

Cathy turned after them, watching the pair of them with a bitter sadness. She remembered similar incidents in the past, times when Anthony had flirted with other girls, particularly when she had argued over something he wanted. Just the implied threat that she could lose him had brought her back into line. But not this time, he no longer had that power over her.

Cathy felt sorry for Jillian. The girl would be exulting in the attention Anthony was giving her, completely unaware that she was merely a pawn to the man she adored. Cathy wished she could tell her the truth but knew the girl would never believe her. Her infatuation would close her ears to anything said against Anthony, particularly by someone whom she perceived as a rival.

With a heavy sigh, Cathy turned back towards the house. The day was going to be even more difficult than she had imagined. She hoped that Anthony would soon be convinced of her lack of interest and leave her alone, but the hope sat uneasily on her. At least with his attention now centred on Jillian, Cathy was free to seek out Tom and talk to him.

He had to listen. She would make him listen, if she could get him alone with her for a while.

CHAPTER ELEVEN

THE wall with which Tom surrounded himself was formidable, far more formidable than Cathy had anticipated. For hours she had watched and waited for an opportunity to speak to him alone, but there had been no opportunity. Not only did Vanessa cling to him like a limpet, but she and Tom were forever in company with others; talking, smiling, laughing. And as he had done last night, Tom simply refused to see Cathy. Whenever she came into his direct line of vision, he looked straight through her, as if she were not there.

There were people everywhere, milling from one group to another. A huge marquee had been erected between the summerhouse and the woolshed, and the large number of men outside it designated this as the main bar. The barbecues and spits were in operation and were popular gathering-spots. A large number of vehicles had been parked in an orderly fashion near the woolshed which was some two hundred metres from the main house. More were still arriving. Several children were skylarking in the pool, and even as Cathy watched, more came running to hurl themselves into the water with gleeful shouts and resounding splashes. Jacko was in attendance, supervising the general hilarity and seeing that no one got hurt.

Cathy was reminded of her own childhood. She

had loved the water, loved swimming. Happy, carefree days, but far, far in the past. She wondered if she would ever feel carefree again, then dismissed the thought. She had to do something about Tom, and waiting around for an opportunity which was not going to come was not doing something.

Tom and Vanessa were stretched out on sun-loungers which had been grouped on the lawn near the pool. Around them was a small party of guests; drinking, eating, making merry. Whether it was a deliberate move on Anthony's part or not, Cathy couldn't guess, but he and Jillian had gathered another party around them on the other side of the pool.

Anthony was making a provocatively public display of his interest in Jillian, but Cathy was not provoked by it. She just wished he weren't in full view of any approach she made to Tom. Anthony could very well decide to complicate matters, and the situation was quite complicated enough without any malicious interference from him.

She saw Vanessa lean over and stroke Tom's arm, and he smiled at her. Cathy's stomach curdled. Tom was so very attractive when he smiled and Vanessa was absolutely basking in his attention. Cathy was beginning to detest the sight of Vanessa with Tom. She had to detach Tom from her, and from everyone else as well. It was imperative.

With frantic resolution in every step she walked down the side of the pool towards him. Her heart fluttered nervously. She desperately tried to control her inner agitation and hoped that her outer composure showed none of it. Step by step she came closer to Tom but he did not look up. Vanessa did and the aquamarine eyes looked hostile.

Cathy faltered for a moment, her mind a frightening blank. What was she going to do or say? Tom said something and the group around him broke into laughter. He sat there like a king amongst his courtiers and they were hanging on his words, just as the guests around the table had done last night.

'Hey! Miss Cathy!'

The shout from Jacko jangled in her ears. Her head jerked around. Jacko's wide grin was beaming at her from the other side of the pool, Anthony's side.

'How about changing for a swim? You can give me a race.'

'I didn't bring a swimming costume with me, Jacko,' she excused herself quickly.

'Plenty of spares in the summerhouse, Cathy,' Anthony called out. 'We'd all like to see you race Jacko.'

'What a good idea!' Vanessa declared eagerly. 'Come on, Cathy! Be a sport and show us your paces. Cathy used to be a State swimming champion,' she announced to all and sundry.

Cathy wished the ground would open beneath her and swallow her up. Everyone was looking at her with expectant interest—everyone except Tom, whose hooded gaze seemed to be fixed on the drink in his hand. The last thing in the world she wanted at this moment was to be the focus of general attention, and she was certainly not going to show off her paces in the swimming-pool, especially not in front of Anthony, who was probably preparing to make some mean-hearted capital out of it.

She turned back to Jacko, forcing an apologetic smile. 'I haven't swum for a long time, Jacko. I wouldn't even be a match for you any more. Thanks for the offer, but not today.'

There was a chorus of disappointed protests led by Anthony and Vanessa, but Cathy simply shook her head and walked determinedly towards Tom. Her cheeks were burning, her heart was a sledgehammer. But if she did not go to him now she doubted she could pluck up the courage to make another approach. She ignored Vanessa, she ignored everyone but Tom. And Tom continued to ignore her until she touched his hand in mute appeal. Only then did he lift his face to her, slowly, reluctantly, and the face was a study in impassive neutrality.

'Tom, I'd like to talk to you,' she blurted out, too flustered to be anything but direct.

His eyes were totally expressionless. He waved a careless welcome. 'Sit down. Be comfortable. Talk away as much as you please.' He swept a dry smile around the present company. 'We're all talkers here.'

'Privately,' she insisted, burning even more painfully with the embarrassment of having had her request drawn to the attention of the others.

'This is hardly the day for private tête-à-têtes,' Tom remarked lightly. 'Be one of the party. Besides, I have no secrets from my companions here. Say what you like—I'm sure we'd all be happy to listen to you.'

His encouraging smile had a touch of grimness that told Cathy more surely than words that he was not going to be moved, not by her, for any reason.

'Perhaps later, at your convenience,' she murmured defeatedly.

'I'm afraid I'm tied up, but when I'm free I'll let you know,' he replied flippantly.

The blood drained from her face. It was the end of the line; Tom wouldn't come to her.

Vanessa laughed with bitchy amusement, rubbing in her mortification. 'You really can't take Tom away from us, Cathy. We all need him here.'

Rejected and publicly humiliated, Cathy was about to turn away when Tom's blasé attitude abrupytly changed. Vanessa's laughter faltered as he swung his legs to the ground and stood up.

'On the other hand,' he said smoothly, 'I'm sure what you have to tell me won't take long.' He swept a smile around the others 'You must excuse me, I'll be back shortly.'

Cathy felt dizzy with relief. He had taken her side, he was coming with her—because of Vanessa's laughter. However bitterly he resented what she had done to him, however much he would inwardly criticise her, he still sprang to her defence when someone else tried to put her down. A little cord of hope vibrated in her heart. Perhaps Tom still loved her enough to forgive what she had done to him. He was coming with her, even taking her arm. Just his touch on her elbow warmed her soul.

She wished she could just turn to him, cling to him, and have his arms come round her, holding her tight. She had always felt safe in Tom's embrace—no, more than safe; cherished. And she desperately wanted to recapture what had been in their relationship. She knew she had to find the right

words, the right actions to persuade Tom to give her
another chance. Her mind stayed completely blank.
She prayed for inspiration.

He stopped walking. Cathy glanced at him in
nervous alarm, hoping to fathom his mood.

'Have we enough privacy here?' he asked in a
bantering tone.

They had reached the outskirts of the crowd, and
clearly he was reluctant to go further with her. Cathy
hesitated, frightened to press him too far. Getting
him away from his party had been like drawing
teeth. Yet she did not want this conversation
overheard or interrupted by anyone. She darted an
agitated glance around and her gaze caught the huge
River Red Gum in the paddock next to the
woolshed. No one was anywhere near it and the
thick-trunked tree with its widely spreading
branches seemed a shady haven away from the
crowd.

'Can we go down there?' she asked, her eyes
pleading for his indulgence.

He hesitated, his face tightening a little, then he
nodded. His hand slipped away from her arm as they
began walking again. Together, but very distinctly
apart, they covered the couple of hundred metres to
the old tree. Every metre made Cathy more and more
conscious of the distance between her and the man at
her side. Her reticence had created it and now words
had to bridge it. But what words?

Tom did not make it any easier for her. He
propped himself against the tree-trunk, thrust his
hands into the pockets of his cream slacks, and faced
her squarely with an air of complete nonchalance.

'What matter is of such gravity that we have to go through this rigmarole?'

His attitude of flippant indifference flustered her. She stared at him, completely tongue-tied, and before her mind could find a suitable reply, his expression changed to harsh mockery.

'Is it to tell me the good news? Is there going to be a wedding? Have you and Anthony set the date?'

'No,' Cathy choked out, appalled and pained by Tom's manner even while recognising that her behaviour had earned it.

His gaze was stony. One eyebrow rose sardonically. 'Is it bad news, then? Anthony doesn't care about you any more. Maybe he prefers them younger, like Jillian.'

He bit the words out with scathing contempt and Cathy instinctively leapt to Jillian's defence, her voice shaking with the memory of all the contempt which had been heaped on her because of Anthony. 'Don't speak about her like that! The poor girl deserves to be pitied for what Anthony is doing to her.' She fired a return attack at him. 'It's so damned easy to make judgements on people, isn't it? They all make such fools of themselves.'

He seemed to withdraw into himself, pasting an impassive mask on his face. 'Yes, you're quite right, they do make fools of themselves. But hopefully they don't keep doing it,' he added bitterly.

He wasn't giving one inch. Cathy sighed and shook her head. The direction the conversation had taken could only be destructive. She had to get it on to more fruitful ground. 'It's not because of them I want to talk to you, Tom.' She lifted eyes which beseeched him to be receptive. 'It's because of us.'

A muscle in his cheek flinched, playing traitor to the mask. His gaze moved to some point beyond her, remained fixed for several long moments, then returned to her, no longer hard, yet strangely detached, as if he had weighed her words in his mind and come to a decision which would not waver.

'No. It's all been said, Cathy. Anything more would be superfluous. I'd only hurt you and you'd only hurt me.'

She felt numb all over. Judgement had been passed. She had to force herself to fight it. 'There is one thing more—a question I have to ask . . .' She swallowed hard, moistening a throat so dry that she thought her voice would crack. Desperation dictated the words. 'What do I have to do to win back your good opinion of me?'

He did not answer. He seemed so still and distant that Cathy wondered if he had heard her. She did not know what else to say. Despair was eating into what little courage she had left. When he finally spoke, it was so softly that the words barely floated across to her.

'There's nothing you can do which can change my opinion of you.'

He was lost to her, irrevocably. Panic clawed at her heart, tearing out words which poured from her mouth with passionate urgency. 'I know I must seem contemptible to you—inconstant, faithless, untrustworthy. God knows I've been a self-centred fool for so long that I'm almost too ashamed to beg it of you, but I am begging, Tom. Give me a chance to prove to you that I'm not what you think.'

There was no reaction from him, none at all. Cathy plunged on, barely knowing what she was saying or whether it made any sense. 'It's all finished with Anthony. If you want to know what he did to me all those years ago, I'll tell you. There's nothing I want to hide from you. You'll probably despise me, but it is a thing of the past, over, behind me. And I've paid dearly for it—far, far too dearly, if it means I've lost you. It's you, Tom, you, that's important to me, no one else.'

He turned a face to her which was curiously blank, wiped of all expression, as was his voice when he spoke. 'If that's so, Cathy, why are we here at Mirrima?'

Flat. Dead. The question which condemned her, judgement passed and ratified. Yet still she could not give up. 'We're at Mirrima because I made a lot of wrong, emotional decisions at a traumatic period of my life. They led to things I couldn't live with. I couldn't even live with myself. So I constructed a new life, a new me. But the scars only faded, they never healed. You said it yourself, Tom—I was an emotional cripple.'

Tears pricked her eyes but she forced herself to go on. 'I was happy with you, Tom. I thought the past was buried until Anthony came and opened it all up again, inviting us to Mirrima. I had to come back here to sort myself out, and in one way, it was the best thing I could have done, because I can now look at what happened squarely in the face and see the reality of what occurred. I never did love Anthony, and he nearly destroyed me to satisfy his own selfish needs.'

She gulped to clear the lump in her throat. Tom was only a blur through the tears in her eyes, but he had not moved. She kept talking. 'It wasn't something I could ever bring myself to speak about. I didn't stop you from coming here because I needed you with me. You belonged to my new life and I needed you as a balance against them ... Anthony and his parents, Mirrima and all it represents. I'm sorry, I couldn't think straight. I know that's no excuse for what I've done.'

Slowly, sadly, she added, 'It would have been better for me to remain an emotional cripple, unless you can forgive me for the hurt I've given you.'

Clumsily she wiped the tears from her eyes with the back of her hand while her mind searched frantically for what to say next.

'There's nothing to forgive, Cathy. Nothing at all.'

Her heart gave a little flutter of hope at the softly spoken words, but one clear look at Tom's face minimised the hope.

He gave her a bleak smile. 'I'm glad you don't love Anthony. He could never have made you happy.'

She took one hesitant step towards him, her hands stretching out in mute appeal. 'Can we be friends again, Tom?'

The bleak smile faded and his face seemed to sag into weariness. 'Yes, we can be friends, in time. But for the present I must go away.'

'Why?'

The question spilled off her tongue before she thought about it and Tom flinched as though he had been hit. His eyes stabbed pain back at her.

'Because I love you too deeply,' he all but

whispered, each word laden with suppressed emotion. 'Because my being near you, seeing you every day . . . it would weigh you down, become oppressive.' He forced a travesty of a smile. 'Do you know how you can make any dog savage? You chain him up, just out of reach of something he desperately wants, something like a big bone with plenty of meat on it. He'll go mad trying to get at it. Being near you would do the same to me. You see, I now know you're unattainable, so I have to go away.'

He pushed himself away from the tree and there was a look of infinite sadness in his eyes. 'Thank you for telling me what you did. It takes a great load off my mind. Please excuse me, Cathy. I can't stay with you any longer.' He turned to go.

Cathy stood motionless, speechless, her whole being concentrated on a message whhich was pulverising her heart, bursting across her brain, finally making sense of everything she had ever felt about Tom. He was already a few paces away when it finally found voice.

'I love you, Tom. I've been trying to tell you that all along. I love you.'

His back went rigid. He stood so still for so long that Cathy herself was frightened to move. She wanted to run to him, throw her arms around him and declare her love over and over again. The sure knowledge of it was washing through her like a tidal wave, sweeping everything else into insignificance. She loved Tom, loved him with her whole being. She pushed aside the reserve of years and ran over to him, but Tom swung on the instant and caught her wrists as she was about to fling her arms around his neck. He forcibly held her off, and the fierce look of rejection on his face denied any further attempt at an embrace.

'It's not enough!' he grated out savagely.

'What ... what do you mean?' she stammered, shaken and bewildered by his reaction. 'I know I've been terribly stupid and hurtful in my blindness, but I do know what I feel now, Tom. I love you. What more can I say?'

He clenched his jaw and shut his eyes. The almost unbearable tension in him was transmitted to her through the hands still grasping her wrists. Cathy could not think what else to say, and she was terribly, terribly frightened that it would not matter what she said. Tom was not prepared to believe her.

His eyes opened to dark slits which glittered with menacing intensity. 'Would you love me in bed, Cathy? Can you say that?'

The words were hissed like stinging whips, words which scourged him as deeply as they scourged her. They both knew she had never given any indication of sexual desire for him. He threw her hands away and with a groan of agony, he turned from her and half staggered over to the tree-trunk. He smashed his fist against the unyielding wood, again and again in a blind, helpless explosion of frustration and rage and need and mindlesss grief.

'You don't want me, Cathy, not that way.' Hoarse words, strained out of a passion driven beyond all restraint, and once more he drew back his fist and hammered it against the tree.

She had to stop him, stop the destructive words and actions. She ran to him and grabbed his hand before he could repeat the stroke. Her strength was no match for his, but on her touch his swing faltered and he half turned towards her.

'For goodness' sake, Tom, stop it! You'll hurt yourself!'

He shook his head, the dark eyes sick with self-torture, his voice close to breaking as he choked out his pain. 'You don't respond to me, not like with him. I could have lived with it if I'd never seen you with Anthony. But in your bedroom yesterday, I saw the look on your faces, in your eyes. I could almost taste the sexual tension between you. You must go your way, Cathy, and you must let me go mine. I can't bear it any longer.

'No, no! I don't want him. I don't, Tom. It was only because of what happened in the past.'

'Don't, Cathy! Don't deny what is, or pretend what isn't,' he cried, and with a groan of hopeless need he pulled her against him and wrapped her in a crushing embrace. His hand pressed her head on to his shoulder and his face rubbed against her hair in an agony of yearning. His chest heaved again and again as if his great heart was fighting against the constriction placed upon it. 'Cathy, as much as I want you, I will not, I cannot, I shall not be second best to any man with my wife. Eventually it would destroy us, both of us.'

She struggled against the despairing inevitability in his words. 'It wouldn't be like that, Tom. We love each other. I love you and you love me. What Anthony had with me wasn't love. It wouldn't even compare to what we could have.' The hand on her head relaxed its hold a little and she thrust it back enough so that she could look into his eyes, frantic to convince him that she spoke the truth. 'I'd do anything I can to make you happy, Tom.'

Slowly, wearily, he closed his eyes to the desperate plea in hers. He seemed to rock unsteadily for a moment, then he loosened his embrace. He stepped back until only his hands were lightly holding her arms and when he opened his eyes, his gaze held a terrible emptiness. His mouth twisted to one side.

'I know you would, Cathy.' He could barely speak, each word an effort that was almost beyond him. 'And both of us would know . . . that you were giving more than love should ever demand.'

'No, it's not true. No, Tom. Please don't think that of me,' she begged, desperate to convince him otherwise but terrified that more words would only feed the monstrous doubt in his mind.

He shook his head. His hands dropped away from her. She knew then, she knew that no man, especially a man who felt as deeply as Tom, could ever live with the thought that the woman he loved could prefer another man as her lover. It hurt too much, was unbearable. Yet there was nothing she could think of which could convince him he was wrong.

'It's not true,' she whispered helplessly.

He did not move. He did not speak. He was so close, yet so very far away. Her heart was bleeding for him, but he was hurting too deeply to accept anything from the woman who had inflicted the pain. Guilt held her silent even while her mind screamed with the need to explain that what she had shared with Anthony was meaningless.

Tom squared his shoulders. His head lifted as he drew in a deep breath. He was gathering the shreds of his dignity together, a proud, strong man whose control had been tested to the limit and beyond. At last he spoke, his voice flat and lifeless and very, very controlled.

'The Lachlans are flying back to Sydney in the morning, and I'm going with them. If you have any feeling for me, Cathy, please leave me alone.' Then he was striding away; fast, hurried, relentless strides, distancing himself from her as quickly as possible.

Cathy stared after him until he disappeared in the crowd. The pain in her heart was more intense than anything she had felt in her life. Her feet started to follow Tom's route, automatically drawn by the need pulsing through her. She suddenly realised what she was doing and halted. She sank down on the grass, feeling faint from the turbulent churning of emotions.

She loved Tom, and she did want all of him, wanted every form of love with him. It was true that she hadn't wanted sex with him. The only sex she had known was sex with Anthony, and she had instinctively shied from repeating that experience. But it wouldn't be the same with Tom. She was sure that sex with love would be very different—a true sharing, not domination and submission but something that would make her feel good and complete, not used.

Too late the desire for Tom stirred in her and took hold. She had just seen a man she had never seen before, a man of great strength who was unbelievably gentle to her; a man of passion, of compassion and integrity, with the simplest of needs—to love fully and be fully loved; a man who stood out from all other men. A man with whom she wanted to share the rest of her life.

She savoured the thought of Tom's body and hers, touching, caressing, joining, holding, becoming one, in love. She closed her eyes and imagined that moment of absolute union with him, and the spasm of need which rippled through her left her in no doubt that she wanted him in every possible sense.

But she had to bide her time now. Somehow she would convince Tom of her love, but not here at Mirrima. Anthony and Mirrima were too closely connected in Tom's mind for her ever to reach through those barriers here. Tomorrow he was leaving with the Lachlans, and then he was going to Italy, away from her altogether if she did not find a way of reaching him.

The Lachlans! Surely if Tom was going with them, their aeroplane had to be at least a four-seater. If she got a lift with them, with Tom, perhaps she could undermine some of his resistance to her and show him that she really did love him, and want him. They would be leaving Mirrima behind, going back to the life they had shared in Sydney, and surely that would help her cause. It was a chance she had to take anyway. There was so little time left to her if Tom was determined on going away.

Cathy climbed to her feet and went in search of the Lachlans. She was not going to lose Tom, not if there was anything in her power to do which would win him back to her.

CHAPTER TWELVE

IT took some considerable time before Cathy could manoeuvre Mary Lachlan aside to make her request, and then she had to apply some rather awkward persuasion. Mary was uncomfortable with the idea of Cathy's taking what she considered a premature leave of Mirrima. While Anthony's attentions to Jillian Barnsworth were far too much in evidence for them to have gone unnoticed, Mary was unconvinced by the abrupt switch of his affections. She offered Cathy some tactful and sympathetic advice, but finally agreed that if Cathy was still intent on leaving when morning came, there would be a seat available for her on the Lachlans' plane.

Cathy thanked her, and sensing that another burst of well-meant advice was teetering on the woman's tongue, she quickly excused herself and slipped away. Mission accomplished, she thought with relief, and for the first time today she was able to relax. Everything was settled, as much as it could be.

Her gaze wandered over the crowd, automatically searching for Tom, but he was nowhere to be seen. He had not returned to Vanessa's party. Cathy sadly reflected that even a man of Tom's strong character would be hard pressed to pretend a convivial mood after the blows she had dealt him. Those blows weighed heavily on her mind, but she countered them with thoughts of tomorrow. Somehow she

would convince Tom of her love and she would make
it up to him for all he had suffered on her account.

Her stomach rumbled its emptiness, reminding
her that she had not eaten since breakfast that
morning. It was now late afternoon and there were
still many long hours to get through before she could
retire for the night. She made her way to the
barbecues, decided she didn't feel like chewing
through a steak and continued on to the spits.

A cheerful, ruddy-faced young man was delighted
to serve her with slices of roast lamb and insisted on
topping them with a couple of potatoes which had
been baked in the hot coals beneath the meat. He
directed her to a small marquee where there was a
large selection of salads, buttered bread and buns,
and urns of tea and coffee. Cathy found she was
surprisingly hungry once she started to eat, and she
felt more ready to face the rest of the party when she
had finished.

As the afternoon shadows lengthened the crowd
drifted down towards the woolshed. Cathy could not
see Tom anywhere, and his prolonged absence
worried her. Anthony was worrying her too. As
much as she tried to avoid and ignore him, he seemed
to follow her around, making opportunities to flaunt
Jillian's devotion to him in Cathy's face.

A Country and Western band arrived and set up
their equipment in the woolshed, and the younger
contingent of the crowd swarmed in, drawn by the
promise of music. Cathy joined the milling group
around the entrance to the huge barn. Here long
tables had been set up, ready for the dispensing of

drinks and fruit salad to those who wanted light refreshment.

The band comprised five musicians and two girl singers, all dressed in the traditional Country and Western style. Their music blared out over amplifiers which were really necessary to carry the sound throughout the huge building. The walls ran up at least two storeys high and the floor space was enormous. Bales of hay had been stacked around the walls for people to sit on when not dancing, and children were climbing up them playing their own games with cheerful disregard for the adults.

Cathy was glad when darkness finally fell; time could not pass quickly enough for her. Floodlights were switched on outside the woolshed but there were pools of shadows where she could stand and not feel conspicuous in her loneliness. She did not want to get involved in the dancing, but it was something to watch while the hours ticked away.

She slowly became aware of being watched herself. Warily she glanced around and was relieved to see Tom in a group of men just beyond the refreshment table. His face was slightly turned away from her, but she did not doubt that it was his gaze she had felt boring into her. She wished she knew what he was thinking and could not help hoping that he was reconsidering their relationship.

The band finished playing another bracket and took a break. There was a sudden surge of people wanting drinks and Cathy briefly lost sight of Tom in the mêlée. Then Vanessa was there, hanging on to his arm obviously trying to cajole him towards the dance-floor. Cathy wryly acknowledged that it had been jealousy souring her view of Vanessa earlier today, but she was not jealous now, only a little envious that Vanessa could claim Tom's attention while she had to hold back. But that was only a matter of time, Cathy assured herself.

The music started up again. Vanessa led Tom inside. Cathy was startled to find herself being swept inside by a smiling stranger who was not about to be refused. 'Let's dance, pretty lady,' he commanded more than asked, and whirled her around with more exuberance than skill. It transpired that he was a grazier from somewhere near Forbes, and when the dance was over, he insisted on carrying her off to introduce her to his group of friends. From then on Cathy was in continual demand as a dancing partner. The company was pleasant enough and it was an easier way of passing the time than standing alone.

However, she grew pricklingly aware that Anthony was not pleased With her popularity on the dance-floor. Several times he deliberately bumped into her, holding Jillian very closely as he apologised very charmingly. But the green eyes glittered another message. Whether it was a warning or a threat, Cathy was not sure, but she was discomfited, and was even more discomfited when the band paused between numbers and Anthony loomed up behind her partner, tapping his on the shoulder.

'Do you mind?' he asked with all his ingrained arrogance.

'She's yours,' the man conceded goodnaturedly, and turned away without a thought for Cathy.

Anthony stepped into his place as the band started

up again. Cathy didn't want to dance with him. Her whole body stiffened with rejection.

'I'd rather sit this one out, Anthony, if you'll excuse me,' she said coldly.

He pulled her into his arms. 'You're not running away from me, Cathy. We're going to sort this out here and now.'

'There's nothing to sort out,' she retorted, struggling to free herself.

'If you want a scene in front of everyone, I'll give it to you!' he hissed in her ear. 'Now dance with me.'

He would do it too—make a public fool of her if she went against him. She gave in, resenting the force he was using but assured that he could not do her any harm in the middle of a crowded dance-floor.

'Forget what happened today, Cathy. It's you I need, the only woman I want. I can't stand that little Barnsworth bitch crawling all over me. You've got to stop denying what we have together, because it is there. You know it and I know it, and I'll be damned if I'll let it go!'

The impassioned words broke over her head like a relentless wave, but Cathy's heart remained as hard and impervious as a rock. 'It's over, Anthony. You have to let it go,' she whispered vehemently.

Frustration and anger glared back at her. 'You're enjoying this, aren't you? You're so damned proud of yourself!'

'I don't know what you mean.'

'Yes, you do. Standing back from me, not satisfying my desires, flaunting your body in front of every man on the dance-floor—teasing, provoking. You really know now to turn the screw, don't you?'

Protest burst from her. 'For God's sake, Anthony! Stop twisting everything. I've hardly been near you all day, and when I was, you only had eyes for Jillian.'

'Got to you, didn't it?' he taunted, a wild triumph in his eyes. 'Made you go a little cold inside?'

'Yes!' she hissed angrily. 'I prayed that you wouldn't use her as you did me, but I suspect that nothing would be able to help her.'

He laughed, and it was a laugh that chilled her.

'When you're like this you know it excites me. Tell me what you want, Cathy. You can have it. I'll do it for you. God, I want you so much!' He pulled her closer, grinding her body against his so that she could not help but be aware of his arousal. 'Feel what you do to me, Cathy.'

Horror froze her for a moment. He was doing it to her again, in the midst of all this crowd. A shudder of revulsion ran through her and she tried to jerk away. He laughed at her reaction and tightened his hold on her.

'You're obscene!' she grated furiously.

'And you love it,' he gloated.

She stared at him for a long moment. There was no talking sense to him; Anthony could not or would not see her from any other point of view but his. 'I'm not dancing any more, Anthony.'

'I don't want to dance either. Let's go.'

'I'm not going anywhere with you,' she retorted hotly, trying once more to push away from him.

'What the hell are you holding out for?' he demanded. 'A marriage proposal? Is that it? You want a public declaration?'

He gave her no chance of reply.

'You can have it. I will marry you. I'll get my father to announce it now, in front of everyone. Will that satisfy you?'

'No!' she gasped, appalled at his total disregard for everything she had said. 'I don't love you, Anthony, and I don't want to marry you. I don't even want to be with you. Will you please understand that and leave me alone?'

His eyes seemed to glaze over with disbelief. 'Are you crazy? It's not only me you're refusing, but all Mirrima! You can't be serious!'

'Mirrima doesn't mean as much to me as it does to you,' she spelled out on a swell of bitterness for the callous sacrifice he had made of her for his beloved property. 'In fact, if you want the truth, it doesn't mean anything to me at all.'

'You're a fool!' he snarled. 'You're just saying that. You want to hurt me. It can't be true. Mirrima is everything.' His voice gathered a note of hysteria, of total disbelief. 'What more can I offer you? What more can anybody want?'

'Love. You wouldn't understand that, Anthony.'

'I love you. How many times do I have to say it?'

She shook her head in exasperation. 'It's not what you say, it's what you mean and do. Forget me, Anthony! Just leave me alone!'

His mouth curled in contempt and he pushed her away. 'I'll leave you alone all right! You're not worth another bloody thought!'

He left her in the middle of the dance-floor and barged his way through the other dancers, not bothering to disguise his black rage. Cathy felt nothing, except possibly relief. She was past caring what Anthony did so long as she was free of him. Nevertheless she was trembling from aftershock and she was still making her own way off the floor when Anthony's father suddenly stepped in front of her.

'My dance, I think,' Carlton said smoothly and gathered her into his arms.

Cathy was too startled to do anything but silently acquiesce. She followed his rather formal dance-steps in a haze of embarrassment. The situation was vastly different from what it had been last night and she had no idea how much Carlton had seen of, or read into, today's events. She felt constrained to break the awkward silence.

'Your party is a huge success. All the organisation has been wonderful.'

He answered matter-of-factly. 'It's almost routine, Cathy. We've been doing it for thirty years. But that isn't what I want to talk to you about.'

He paused and Cathy tensed. With all the shocks she had had since coming to Mirrima she did not know what to expect from Carlton now. She glanced sharply up at him and was surprised to find soft apology in his eyes.

'I was wrong about you, Cathy, all those years ago. I wish . . . well, never mind about that. We made a bad mistake.' He sighed and continued. 'I don't understand what's going on between you and Anthony. I don't want to know. That's your business. As far as I'm concerned, I'm glad you've made a success of your life, and I want you to know you'll be welcomed here at Mirrima any time you want to come. My wife and I . . . we'd both welcome you.'

The bitter irony of his welcome choked her for a moment. Five years ago those words would have meant the world to her; now they meant nothing. 'Thank you for your kindness but I won't be coming back to Mirrima, Carlton,' she said stiffly.

'Don't be hasty now,' he chided quickly. 'All lovers have their spats.'

She took a deep breath and spelled out the truth. 'We're not lovers, Carlton, not this time. It was memories that brought me back here. I don't love Anthony, and I told him so this morning. And he doesn't love me. I don't believe he ever did.'

Carlton stiffened slightly. 'I see. Then he's not just trying to make you jealous with the Barnsworth girl.'

Cathy made no reply.

'Well, it's none of my business,' he sighed, and they finished the dance in silence.

The conversation had depressed her, and the accumulated strain of the day depressed her even further. Enough was enough. She was fed up with Mirrima and everything it entailed, and she did not owe it or its owners any more of herself. Tom was the only person to whom she owed anything.

Her gaze searched for him as she walked out of the woolshed. He was there, in the same group of men gathered beyond the refreshment tables. Cathy went straight up to him and claimed his attention, ignoring the reserve in his eyes.

'Tom, I've arranged to go back to Sydney with the Lachlans. I'm sorry that it has to be with you when you don't want me, but I can't stay here, not without you.'

She did not wait for a reply, but walked on, half

blinded by a sudden rush of tears and intent on reaching her room so that she could shut out the misery that was Mirrima. She blundered past rows of cars, heading in the general direction of the house. When she finally lifted her head to check for the shortest route, another shock hit her so hard that she faltered in her step and stood pinned to the spot.

Anthony was sitting in the back seat of the next car. Jillian's blonde head was moving slowly across his bare shoulder. Cathy gritted her teeth. How could he use the girl's feeling for him so callously, just to feed his ego! But when had Anthony ever really cared about anyone's feelings but his own! Cathy forced herself to move, to run, from the present as well as the past.

'Cathy!'

Anthony's voice. Panic made Cathy stumble. Anthony had seen her. A car door opened and slammed. He was coming after her. A girl's cry— Jillian calling. Cathy's heart was pumping under unbearable distress. She couldn't cope with another scene with Anthony. She cried out in fear as he caught her and spun her around. His face was wildly contorted.

'Let me go!' she shrieked.

He shook her. 'You don't want me to let you go, Cathy. You came after me. You know it doesn't mean anything with Jillian. That's only sex, not love.'

'Anthony, what's going on?' A hurt wail from the girl.

'You just stay there!' he snapped back at her.

Outrage tore from Cathy's tongue. 'Don't treat her

like that! How can you be so cruel when she . . . when she'd do anything for you? How can you?'

Anthony shook her again. 'Because she doesn't count. Only you, Cathy. It's you I love.'

'No! You don't love anyone but yourself. And I hate you! I hate you for what you've done to me and I hate you for what you're doing to Jillian. I never want to see you again!'

She had spat the words out recklessly, too worked up to consider how Anthony might react, but the moment she stopped her wild tirade, she knew she had unleashed the beast in him, the dark, terrible side that she had sensed but never really seen clearly.

'Hate me, then, but I'll have you, Cathy.' His voice shook with rage. 'No other man will ever have you. I'll give you something that will remind you of me for ever!'

Sheer terror gave her the strength of a cornered animal. She wrenched herself out of Anthony's hold and plunged away from him, stumbling straight into another obstacle, a broad muscular chest. Two strong arms enfolded her quivering body, and a voice was speaking . . . Tom's voice, cold, impersonal, implacable, deadly.

'Give me an excuse, any excuse at all, and I'll beat you to a pulp, Anthony. I'll break every major bone in your body. Nothing could give me greater satisfaction. Just give me the excuse.'

Relief pumped through Cathy's distraught mind. Her arms wound around Tom and clung desperately. She dropped her head on to his shoulder and laid all her weight against him, instinctively giving herself into his keeping.

Anthony laughed.

A convulsive shudder ran through Cathy. Tom's arms tightened around her, secure, protective arms, assuring her of safety.

'Take her, Tom. I won't fight you for her. I'd never fight for her,' jeered Anthony. 'I've had all I want of her, and spoiled her for any other man. You're welcome to what's left!'

His diabolical malevolence had the force of a deadly blow. Cathy's knees gave way and she sagged.

Tom supported her. 'It's all right, Cathy,' he murmured soothingly. 'I'll take you to your room.'

'Yes, take her away, Tom. You can have her. Marry her. And while you sleep, and she lies awake at your side, wanting my touch, I'll know I've won,' Anthony taunted maliciously. 'For she will, Tom. She'll never be able to forget me, or love you.'

Cathy closed her eyes in sick defeat. Anthony was poisoning Tom's mind against her just when he had come back to her, when she needed him so badly, when she knew she loved him and couldn't bear to live without him. And Anthony was destroying it all, killing any trust which could have arisen between them, isolating her, alone in an empty, empty world.

'No!' It was a groan of anguish. Then even as a mortally wounded prey would turn on its hunter, she twisted in Tom's arms and faced her tormentor. 'No, no, no!' she screamed in tortured defiance.

Anthony laughed, triumphant. 'Oh, she's good, Tom, really good. I had her last night. She was screaming yes then, begging me to do anything I wanted with her.'

Cathy's brain snapped. 'You liar! You liar!' she shrieked from the despairing depths of her soul.

Tom drew her head back on to his shoulder and spoke calmly and coldly. 'I know you're lying, Anthony. Cathy brought me to Mirrima with her for one purpose only, and that was to look after her. And I did that. I was with Cathy last night—all night. And neither you nor I slept with her.'

Cathy could hardly believe her ears. Tom saying that? Understanding burst across her dazed mind. Tom believed her. He believed her and he was bluffing Anthony, denying him his triumph, diminishing the power of his lies, and standing up for her. She ached with love for him as he continued his defence of her, a defence which was also an attack.

'I didn't leave Cathy until morning and then I had a few hours' sleep in my own room, which was why I was so late down to breakfast. And I'll swear to that, on oath, in a court of law. If you repeat one word of what you've just said about Cathy, I'll have you charged with defamation of character, and the damages will not be large. They will be punitive.'

The silence which followed Tom's declaration held a strange, tense stillness. The gauntlet had been thrown down. Would Anthony dismiss it? He could not know whether Tom was telling the truth. The only certainty was that Tom was not going to back down. Cathy could feel him pulsing with aggression, all stoked and primed to take Anthony on in any kind of fight. She held her breath, waiting, hoping, willing Anthony to give up and back off.

The music from the woolshed drifted across the eerie stillness. It seemed far away, from another world. Closer, much closer was the pitiful sound of dry, wrenching sobs . . . Jillian's sobs. And right in Cathy's ears was the fearful thumping of her own heart.

It was Tom who finished it, calmly and succinctly. 'So now we all know you're a liar, Anthony. In case you have any more bright ideas, I'll be spending tonight with Cathy too. Right up until the time we leave Mirrima tomorrow morning with the Lachlans. Do you think you can walk, Cathy?'

'Yes,' she whispered. She would make herself walk anywhere to get away from Anthony, to go anywhere with Tom.

Tom curled his arm protectively around her shoulders and he moved her with him, walking up to the house, the Mirrima homestead, so beautiful, so old, so laden with ugly memories.

'She's not worth it, Tom!' Anthony yelled after them, his lacerated ego goading him to have the last word. 'Not worth the time or the trouble!'

Cathy shivered. Tom hugged her closer. He did not turn back or reply. They kept on walking.

CHAPTER THIRTEEN

CATHY felt numb. She knew this was the end. There was no possible hope left. The malevolence of Fate and Anthony's poisonous malice had conspired against her. No man would remain unscathed by the verbal punishment Anthony had handed out tonight. Even though Tom had stood up for her, he had already been harbouring the doubts that Anthony had fed. He could never want her again—no man would. They were walking together, but away from the life they could have shared.

One night, that was all she had left. Tom had said he would stay the night with her, to protect her from Anthony. Was there any possible chance of reconciliation? She darted a glance at his face, but it was as still and composed as if it had been carved out of marble, an immovable quality that crushed any vestige of hope. No word had been spoken and Cathy knew the situation was beyond words, but the helpless agony in her mind kept reciting, please don't leave me, please don't go.

They reached the house. In her blind despair she stumbled on the front step, all her weight falling on Tom as she tried to regain her footing. He held her, steadied her, then in one seemingly effortless swoop, he dropped his arm to her waist, slid his other arm under her buckling knees, and lifted her up, cradling her against his chest. Instinctively Cathy flung an arm around the great breadth of his back, the other encircling his neck, and laid her head against his, grateful for the chance to cling on to him, to be this close to him for the little time before Tom put her down again.

It felt so good. Cathy shut her eyes and savoured the strength and the gentleness of the man she loved, storing away the precious memory. One short night and then he would be lost to her. His footsteps rang loudly on the parquet floor of the great hall, echoing, amplifying the sound of emptiness. And Cathy knew there would be a terrible emptiness in her life without Tom. Her hold on him tightened in convulsive need.

Tom readjusted her position as he started up the grand staircase, and she was swept by a wave of guilt. It wasn't fair to let him keep carrying her. She was no lightweight and he had to be finding it a strain. She lifted her head, reluctant to part from him but forcing herself to speak.

'Tom, you can put me down. I can walk.'

He paused and turned his gaze on her, a dark, turbulent gaze which slowly roved over the pinched whiteness of her face, probed the sick yearning in her eyes, then took on a steady gleam of decisive purpose. 'I think I prefer it my way.' And pressing her even closer to him he continued on up the stairs.

A tingle of life stirred in the hope which had seemed so completely dead. Why did Tom want to carry her? His hold on her felt possessive, and there had been no contempt in his look, no dismissal, no evasion. He had been searching for something, coming to a decision, and he had not let her go.

Nor did he let her go at the top of the stairs. He was breathing heavily but on he went, down the hallway, into her bedroom, and kicked the door shut, still not loosening his hold on her. Dear God, Cathy prayed, let me have a miracle. Let him still want me. And her heart beat out the prayer in a wild drum of hope.

He did not bother with the light switch, but the room was not in darkness. The curtains which Tom had opened the day before had not been drawn and moonlight streamed through the window. There was a moment when he paused, clutching her even more tightly, his chest heaving with exertion, and she was not sure if the pounding heart she felt was hers or his. Then he carried her over to the four-poster bed and gently laid her down.

Cathy clung on to him, afraid that if she let him go, the miracle would turn into a mirage. Tom did not resist, he remained bending over her. His hand brushed the curls from her forehead and he pressed a kiss on it.

'It's all right, Cathy. It will be all right now,' he murmured reassuringly.

She could hardly dare believe what was happening. Tom was not rejecting her. But she didn't want a kiss on her forehead, she wanted so much more. Her arms were around his neck. He made a slight movement to pull away and she hung on with all her strength.

'Tom.'

'Yes?'

He was so close. Her eyes drank in the softness in his, imploring them to stay soft for her. 'You said you wouldn't leave me tonight. I don't want you to leave me.'

'I won't leave you, I promise.'

And he carried the promise to her quivering lips, stilling the fear inside her with a kiss so gentle, but so infinitely sweet that the hope in Cathy's heart blossomed into a beautiful, fragile flower, tremulous in its shape, vulnerable to hurtful mistakes, but there to be nurtured if only it got the right encouragement. She sucked in a quick breath as Tom's mouth left hers. She had to speak, clear away any doubts.

'Tom, it wasn't true, what Anthony said tonight.' Quick, anxious, pleading words.

He placed a hushing finger on her lips and the eyes that looked into hers were filled with another question, far more intense than the one on her mind. 'This afternoon you said you loved me.' It was barely a murmur, yet the words throbbed with emotion.

'I do. I do love you, Tom,' she whispered, and the whisper itself was a breath of love.

'Then whatever Anthony might say is of no consequence.'

No consequence. It didn't matter to him. She shuddered with relief as she pushed aside the ugliness of that last confrontation with Anthony. 'Will you hold me? Hold me close, Tom? I've been so frightened you wouldn't believe me, that you wouldn't want me any more.'

His weight came down on the bed, tipping her towards him even as his arms went around her, hugging her close. She lay half across him as he stroked her hair and back with long, soothing caresses. It was wonderful to rest her head on his chest, to feel his body warmth and the steady rhythm of his breathing. She was filled with a contentment she had never known before, as if suddenly, after years of tramping a wilderness, she had come home, and home was the most wonderfully comforting place in the world.

'I did a lot of thinking after I left you,' Tom said softly. 'And the one conclusion I kept coming to was that if you loved me in any way at all, then I'd take whatever you were prepared to give me. I decided to tell you when you came back to Sydney, after we'd both left Mirrima behind and could be close again. But when you told me tonight you'd be leaving with the Lachlans tomorrow, there seemed no point in waiting, so I followed you.'

She levered herself up and pressed her cheek to his, snuggling closer to his body, sighing with the pleasure of being able to lie with him like this. 'You don't know how grateful I am that you did. I couldn't bear the thought of losing you, Tom,' she whispered. 'I think I would have followed you to Italy if I couldn't change your mind about us before you went.'

His breathing seemed to come more quickly and his hand came up to cover hers, holding it against his chest, their fingers intertwining, until suddenly he heaved himself on to his side, leaning over her, looking down at her. His hand lifted, smoothing back her hair so that her face was open to him, and Cathy waited, all attention tightly concentrated on the searching dark eyes. And it seemed a long, long time before he spoke.

'Come to Italy with me, Cathy! Let's go anyway.

Just the two of us, a new beginning.'

'Yes,' she said without hesitation, and wound her arms around his neck, pulling him down to her, half lifting herself, arching her body to his.

His arms slid around her, catching her closer as his mouth met hers, exploring all the nuances of pressure and taste, lovingly, a giving and a return of the giving, a poignant awareness in their kiss which had never been in any other, and neither of them wanted it to end. Even when their mouths parted there was only a whisper of breath between them.

Then Tom was raining kisses all over her face in a driven burst of emotion. 'Cathy, Cathy, Cathy!' Her name was a prayer of adoration, a passionate need, a primitive mating-call; and when his mouth took hers again it was with a long, desperate hunger which fired the same hunger in her.

She felt the stirring of primeval need, a sense of climbing exultation; the intimacy of the kiss awoke a trembling anticipation. This man was the man she had been made for, the one her soul cried out for, the one her body craved for to give her life completion.

Her hand slid under the collar of his open-necked shirt, savouring the muscular strength of his shoulder, strength that had been used on her behalf tonight. And the great heart which drove the strength leaped under her touch as her hand wandered down, feeling, relishing, wanting. Her own pulse raced to match his, an exultant beat of togetherness; a togetherness all the more precious for having been almost sundered. Then inexplicably Tom was ending the kiss, the pressure of his lips lessening, retreating from her.

He was moving away from her, moving his body away as well, so that she could not feel the hard evidence of his arousal. For a few moments Cathy was too stunned and shaken by the abrupt separation to think. Only slowly did understanding thread into her mind, and it shook her even further. Tom was trying to regain control. His eyes were glazed, his breathing ragged, but he would not pressure her, would not take her; perhaps even believing what Anthony had said, that he would not be a better lover for her.

Her mind screamed a protest at the thought. She could not let Tom doubt her or doubt himself. Her whole body was aching for him, wanting him in a way she had never wanted Anthony, nor would want any other man. Surely he had felt that? But if he hadn't, she had to show him, make him know it beyond any doubt.

She moved on the instant, scrabbling on to her knees beside him, undoing her skirt, lifting off her T-shirt and throwing her bra aside. She grabbed the arm which had cradled her body and lifted his hand to spread his fingers over the swell of her breasts.

'Feel my heart, Tom,' she ordered huskily. 'It beats for you, no one but you.'

'Cathy . . .' It was a strangled groan of need. His head gave a little shake of incredulity even as his eyes drank in the naked fullness of her breasts, clearly delineated in the moonlight. His hand moved, gliding softly over her nipples.

They tautened under the light caress and Cathy shivered with pleasure. But she wanted more than the touch of his hand. She wanted the pressure of his flesh against hers, flesh merging, becoming one, as she had envisaged it this afternoon. She leaned into his hand, encouraging him to take all he wanted while her fingers moved fast to undo the buttons on his shirt and push it aside.

Her touch on his trouser-belt jerked Tom upwards, on to his knees beside her, and his arms came round her in a crushing embrace. 'Cathy, I won't be able to stop unless we stop now,' he muttered hoarsely.

'I don't want to stop.'

For a long, tense moment his embrace almost squeezed the breath out of her. Then in feverish haste he lowered her to the pillows, tore off his shirt, and slid down beside her, his hand cupping one breast with yearning tenderness, his eyes burning with intense need. 'Are you sure, Cathy? Do you want this as much as I do?'

She ran her hands over the heaving muscles of his chest in exultant ownership, up behind his neck, fingers thrusting into his hair, pressing him down to her. 'Yes, Tom, I do,' she assured him with all her love for him throbbing in her voice.

The words had barely left her mouth when he took her face in his hands, his mouth upon hers, claiming that love as his own, taking because he knew it was there for him, and the knowledge stirred a different passion, a certainty, an elation, a freedom which knew no bounds. One hand slid beneath her shoulders, lifting her a little as his mouth trailed to her throat. Cathy arched her neck backwards, wanting every kiss he would give her, savouring every touch of his lips. They moved down, and a hand curved around her breast, shaping it to his mouth, and she trembled uncontrollably as he explored it with his tongue.

Her flesh leapt in little spasms of need when he seemed to pull away from her again. Her eyes flew open in alarm. But he was still there, his hands taking hold of her waistband, drawing her clothes down, discarding them. Featherlight fingers caressed the long length of her legs, and in a strangely moving act of homage, Tom lowered his head and pressed his cheek to her softly rounded stomach. 'You are so beautiful, Cathy. So very beautiful,' he murmured.

With a sigh of reluctance he rose swiftly. She watched him undress, silently marvelling at the majestic strength of the man in his nakedness, and a melting warmth stirred inside her in anticipation of the moment when he would be hers. She stretched out a hand and touched him. 'You're beautiful too,' she whispered.

He knelt over her for a moment, as if savouring the wonder of what was happening. She lifted her arms to him and he came to her, gathering her to him, kissing her over and over, covering her body with kisses, until there was no part of her which was not sensitised to his touch. A tiny voice in her mind was telling her to do things, to pleasure him as he was pleasuring her, to show him how much she wanted him. It was impossible. Her body was quivering so violently she had no control over it any more. Her hands tried to tell him, for she was beyond words. They closed convulsively over his shoulders, imparting to him her urgent need.

She gasped as Tom pressed that first intimate

touch, aching need in conflict with her aroused sensitivity. Before he could hesitate for fear of hurting her, she drew him towards her. He entered her slowly, ripples of pleasure and release growing into a great surge of fulfilment. This fusion of their bodies was so right, so perfect, and as they became one entity, wave after wave of ecstasy trembled through her body.

She clasped him in her arms, hugging him closer, closer. Time ceased to have meaning, ceased to exist as they rolled and moved together, speaking to each other without speech, knowing without having to reveal. It was like a dream, a dream of love that went on for ever.

All night they made love, beyond satiety, beyond languor, tasting an experience which had been waiting for them for too many years. At times they slept, still locked together in this wondrous union, and at times throughout the night they woke as one. There was no need left, no pulsating desire, yet the mutual feeling that this should go on was unabated. And they loved with new, deeper nuances each time. Cathy had never even dreamt that it was possible to share, to know, to understand, to be as one with another human being as it was with Tom this night. It awed and amazed her.

'There are no words to describe it,' he murmured to her once, and she shook her head and kissed him to tell him she felt the same.

So they slept and loved and slept again, and when the sun came up in the morning, they made love once more. Afterwards she lay on top of him, hugging him close, not wanting to be parted from him, saddened that the morning had come.

His fingers feathered up and down her spine. 'Tired?' he asked softly.

The dream was over. Cathy stirred and lifted herself enough to see his face. He was smiling, a beautiful, warm love in his eyes, and he looked wonderfully handsome, even with a stubble of beard and his hair all rumpled.

Cathy smiled too. 'In a way. But not in a sleepy way. Kind of like my mind has never been so sharp. It's a funny feeling.'

'I know. It's marvellous. Like you could go out and conquer the world.'

'Don't do that. I need you to stay here with me.'

'I want to, but we'll have to move soon if we're leaving with the Lachlans. However grateful I should be to Mirrima for leading you to me, my inclination is to take you away as soon as possible, in case you change your mind.'

'Mmm,' she agreed, and snuggled back down to savour what little time they had left. 'I'll never change my mind.'

He laughed. 'Remind me to break this bed before we leave.'

Startled, she raised her head again. 'Whatever for?'

Tom's grin was boyishly triumphant. 'Oh, it'll just give Anthony something to ponder on for the rest of his life.'

The thought tickled her mind. It was absurd and beautiful at the same time, telling her there was no longer any shade of doubt in Tom's mind, that the past was behind them. Her smile was full of contentment. 'You can't do that, Tom. It's an irreplaceable antique. Besides, who's Anthony?'

She felt his laughter bubble up even before he gave vent to it, and when he finished laughing, his eyes still danced with it. 'You're right—there's no one else in the whole world but you.'

'And you.'

When pressure of time finally forced them to move from the bed, Cathy no longer minded. Nothing was ever going to separate her from Tom.

CHAPTER FOURTEEN

'I WILL always love Florence. Of all the places we've been, this is the best,' murmured Tom, and smiled his lazy, slow smile at Cathy.

They lay on the bed, naked, completely sated with their lovemaking. It was early afternoon, hot and humid, and languor filled their veins, making them semi-drowsy. Cathy was totally relaxed, happy and contented, and her smile held an even deeper happiness as Tom softly stroked her stomach. She knew what he meant. When something felt as good as this, you would always remember the place where it happened. Any allusion to it would always bring back wonderful memories.

'Thomas Henry Crawford the Fourth,' Tom sighed with all the pride of paternity.

'It could be a daughter,' Cathy reminded him.

'Well, maybe I'll love Catherine Anne Crawford the Second even more, if she's like her mother.' His gaze ran slowly up her body, lingering for a moment on her slightly swollen breasts before lifting to meet her eyes. 'It's a pity that no one's invented a time machine.'

'What would you do with a time machine? Sell holidays?'

'No. I'd go back about five hundred years and I'd commission Michelangelo to sculpt you in marble, just as you are now, the perfect embodiment of all womanhood. I wouldn't care if he took years to complete it. I could feast my eyes on you for so much longer.'

'I think you'd get hungry in the interim!'

'Yes.' His eyes danced at her, recalling the hunger of their desire only an hour before.

She smiled. 'I doubt that I'd like it in marble. It always seems so very cold and impersonal.'

'But immortal. I'd like to immortalise you like this. Still, if you preferred, I'd get Leonardo as well and he could paint you. They both lived in Florence in the early fifteen-hundreds.'

'Then you can keep the marble. I'll have the painting.'

His hand trailed up to make lazy circles around her breasts. 'I can see there'd be a problem. I don't think either work would ever be completed. Being men, they would certainly be completely distracted. Incidentally, I bought some postcards of that Madonna by Leonardo that we saw in the Uffizi this morning.'

'The Virgin with Flowers?'

'Mmm. Thought we could send one each to our parents—share the joy around. Unless you want to keep it a secret for a while?'

She knew that Tom was bursting to tell everyone and she would never deny him any pleasure. 'That was a nice thought. We'll send them off tomorrow.'

With a sigh of utter contentment he slid an arm under her shoulders and settled down beside her, pressing a light kiss on her hair. 'I've never felt so complete. And yet it's like a rebirth, a renewal of life, a wish to be the best father any child ever had.

Strange, I would have said a couple of months ago, that it was impossible to love anyone more totally than I did you, Cathy, but now my feeling for you is so much richer, deeper.'

'I feel like that too,' she murmured happily.

'I'll let you go to sleep. An expectant mother needs a lot of rest.' There was silence for a minute and then another sigh and a kiss on her hair. 'He'll be a better man than I am, Cathy.'

'Who?'

'Thomas Henry Crawford the Fourth.'

'Why do you say that?'

'Because you're his mother.'

She snuggled closer to him and curved a possessive arm around his waist. 'No one could be a better man than you are, Tom.'

And to Cathy's mind it was absolutely true. Her thoughts drifted back to that traumatic weekend at Mirrima. It really was a different life ago, all the years that had finally come to an end there. Since then she had been unbelievably happy with Tom and he had done the most wonderful things for her . . . lending Barbara the finance so that she could buy half the business and relieve Cathy of any worries about it while she was away, effecting a reconciliation with her parents.

Only God knew how he had talked her father around, but both her parents had come to the wedding, her mother in floods of happy tears, her father stiff and awkward but prepared to accept Cathy back into the family fold. The news of the baby would give them joy. She might never be really close to her father again, but she was no longer an outcast, and for that she was intensely grateful to Tom.

Grateful for so many other things too; uncountable. All she could really do for him was love him and give him children. An indulgent smile curved her lips. He was so happy about the baby. So was she, but Tom's happiness meant more to her right now. She hugged him in an excess of emotion.

'I love you, Tom,' she whispered into his shoulder.

He rubbed his warm mouth over her hair. 'Love you.' It was a soft echo of absolute contentment.

And for all the years of their lives together, whenever Florence was mentioned, their eyes would meet, sharing a secret understanding, and they would smile a very special smile of love.

Harlequin Presents

Coming Next Month

Take 4 best-selling love stories FREE
Plus get a FREE surprise gift!

ATTRACTIVE, SPACE SAVING BOOK RACK

Display your most prized novels on this handsome and sturdy book rack. The hand-rubbed walnut finish will blend into your library decor with quiet elegance, providing a practical organizer for your favorite hard-or soft-covered books.

Only $9.95

Approximately
16" x 8"
when assembled

Assembles in seconds!

To order, rush your name, address and zip code, along with a check or money order for $10.70* ($9.95 plus 75¢ postage and handling) payable to *Harlequin Reader Service*:

> Harlequin Reader Service
> Book Rack Offer
> 901 Fuhrmann Blvd.
> P.O. Box 1325
> Buffalo, NY 14269-1325

> *Offer not available in Canada.*

*New York residents add appropriate sales tax.

BKR-1R

JULIE ELLIS

**author of the bestselling
Rich Is Best rivals the likes of
Judith Krantz and Belva Plain with**

THE ONLY SIN

It sweeps through the glamorous cities of Paris, London, New York and Hollywood. It captures life at the turn of the century and moves to the present day. *The Only Sin* is the triumphant story of Lilli Landau's rise to power, wealth and international fame in the sensational fast-paced world of cosmetics.

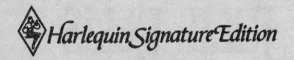
Harlequin Signature Edition

Carole Mortimer

Merlyn's Magic

She came to him from out of the storm and was drawn into
his yearning arms—the tempestuous night held a magic
all its own.

You've enjoyed Carole Mortimer's Harlequin Presents
stories, and her previous bestseller, *Gypsy*.

Now, don't miss her latest, most exciting bestseller,
Merlyn's Magic!

IN JULY